DEATH TAKES A FLYER

a novel by

Barbara J. Olexer

Joyous Publishing
Milwaukie, Oregon, U.S.A.

16-point Large Print

ISBN 0-9722740-3-0
Library of Congress Control Number
2003094986

Joyous Publishing
9752 SE 43rd Avenue, Unit D
Milwaukie, Oregon 97222-1717
www.joyouspub.com

Printed in the U.S.A.

This book is dedicated to

Earl and Dorothy Spivey
and
Robert and Theresa Kennedy

in honor of our friendships that began in
Camp Five in 1952

"There's nothing worth the wear of winning
But laughter and the love of friends."
Hilaire Belloc

Cover photograph by
Laurel Belle French Crawford
from the author's collection

by Barbara J. Olexer

NONFICTION

Presidential Education: Prelude to Power
The Enslavement of the American Indian
in Colonial Times
Murder of a Soul: The Story of
Captain Jack (screenplay)
What Astrology Means to You: A Handbook of
Astrological Terms, Glyphs, and Applications

FICTION

They Lived Ever After
Death Takes a Flyer
Murder by Accident
If You Can't Trust Your Uncle Sam
Father to the Man
Fossil Rocks
Criminal Justice

Chapter 1

I had been restless all day, unable to settle into my usual rhythm for a school day. Maybe because it was Halloween or maybe because the moon was full. The children were excited, of course. I taught the upper four grades of our little two-room school; it was my first job after graduation from college. There were two eighth graders, three seventh graders, four sixth graders, and the Miller twins in the fifth grade. The lower four grades were smaller and my colleague, Mrs. Ziegler only had seven pupils in her room.

The school was the largest building in a logging camp belonging to the mill town of Kinzua. Not only did it house the two schoolrooms but also the large room that did double duty as the gymnasium for the school and the community hall for the camp. I don't think all of the approximately one hundred residents had ever gathered in the community hall but there would have been room for them if they had.

A storm was building and it felt like it would be a big one. Here in the tag end of the Blue Mountains of Oregon, we nearly always had snow on the ground by Halloween but the autumn had been unusually mild this year. I gave each class a reading assignment and went to one of the windows. The tamaracks shown golden bright against the evergreen-covered hillsides. The dark clouds pressed close to the earth, and as I watched, the first flakes of snow drifted slowly down -- big, fluffy, downy flakes. They melted as they touched the ground but I knew they would soon begin to stick.

There wasn't much to do in Camp Five in the evenings in the exact middle of the 20th century. Radio reception wasn't very good and there was no cafe or tavern or malt shop. In fact, except in *Archie* comic books, I had never seen a malt shop with a long marble counter and tables along the sides, with the center clear for dancing to the juke box. There was a Confectionery in Kinzua but it was built on much more modest lines and had no juke box. So Halloween was a major excitement and even the four high schoolers in camp would go trick or treating. At least the three underclassmen would, presumably the lone senior would consider herself too grown up for trick or treating.

We had our Halloween party the last thing in the

afternoon. We could hear the lower four grades having their party while the seventh and eighth grades were supposed to be quietly doing their reading assignments and the fifth and sixth grades were having an oral geography lesson. I had combined the fifth and sixth grades for some lessons so the Miller twins wouldn't always be competing only against each other. Not that Ray Troupe, Doreen Cranston, and Bobby Cabusap were much actual competition but it did dilute the mix. So we plowed through the rivers and lakes and mountains of Africa, not, I'm afraid, fixing any of them very firmly in their minds. Finally, Marie Allston and Eloise Troupe, this year's upper grades room mothers, brought the refreshments and the kids were relieved to be allowed to put their work away and give their whole attention to Halloween.

Marie and Eloise set out the cupcakes with orange frosting and licorice cut to make jack-o'lantern faces and the orange Kool-Aid. Ray Troupe and Debbie Miller fetched a washtub and some of the others carried buckets of water to fill it so the kids could duck for apples. The excitement rose steadily as we played games until 3:30 when they burst through the door into the coatroom, snatched up coats and caps and spilled out onto the playground in a shouting, raucous horde that seemed much more numerous than just eleven. Marie and Eloise and I cleaned up and mopped up the water from the apple bobbing. Florence Granville was the school janitor at that time but we didn't want to leave the extra work for her. Besides Delphine, in the first grade, Florence had four more children, all pre-schoolers. She had plenty of work already.

Walking home, I thought back over the day, the children's noise ceasing abruptly as they scattered to their homes, the farthest about the distance of two city blocks, although the camp wasn't laid out in blocks, from school. There hadn't been anything special about the day other than the Halloween party: Lyle Allston and Ray Troupe had gotten into a fist fight at morning recess. That was nothing remarkable, they fought on an average of about once a week and had managed to damage each other only to the extent of an occasional black eye or bloody nose. Doreen Cranston had irritated me by her incessant whispering and giggling but that was certainly nothing new.

My home was a one-bedroom cabin in the center of camp. The company allotted homes on the basis of status and unmarried schoolteachers didn't rate very high. The biggest house in camp was occupied by the boss of one of the logging "sides." The company ran two sides and those bosses and the foreman of the construction crew rated the best houses. Carl Chichester had claim on the best house by right of seniority. He had worked for the company for sixteen years, the last nine of them as woods boss. Cat-skinners, jammer-operators, and mechanics were high status; timber-fallers and choker-setters were low status. Married men took precedence over bachelors. The bachelors lived in two-man bunkhouses in the upper end of camp and rarely mixed with the families.

All the buildings in camp were wooden frame with board and bat siding. They were all painted brown with white trim and tall old ponderosa pines were scattered around. It was a pretty little place and reminded me of those pictures of New England villages so beloved of calendar makers, although there was no church, much less a church with a high white steeple. There was a little squared-off cupola for a bell on the schoolhouse, though, there was no bell.

My home was as well furnished as any and better than most. When my parents were killed in a boating accident my senior year of college, I had inherited the house in Heppner and most of the furniture. My brother and sister were both older than me and already had their own homes. I had brought the necessities and not much more to camp. There just isn't a lot of space for furniture in two small rooms. I had pretty curtains at the windows and scatter rugs on the floor and my oil stove kept the house toasty warm even in the coldest weather. My only real gripe about my living quarters was the lack of a bathroom. There were several bathroom-less cabins in camp so there was a communal bath house, divided so the sexes each had its own side. It wasn't that far from my door but in cold weather it was extremely inconvenient.

The company often furnished the lumber for people to build onto their company-owned homes but I had been refused permission to add a bathroom to my house. It wasn't the lumber or expense that was at issue; I had offered to pay all expenses myself. It was a question of the sewer system. It seems as if the sewer system, such as it was -- I was afraid to inquire into the exact meaning of that phrase -- was already at capacity.

I dumped the papers I'd brought home to grade on the table and turned up the heat. There was no point in wasting oil on heating an empty house so I turned it way down when I left for school in the mornings. It only took a few minutes to warm the place, it was so small. I built a fire in the trash burner so I would have hot water. Very few of the houses had electric hot water heaters, most of us had reservoirs heated with wood fires. This was not a problem in the winter but in the summer it wasn't so great. I fussed around, putting my coat away and putting on the kettle so I could make some tea, smoothing the knitted afghan on the back of the couch. A little while later I was sitting at the table, correcting math quizzes and sipping my tea when someone knocked on the door.

"Come in," I called.

The door opened and Richanne Worley came in. Richanne is ten years or so older than me but we've always been pretty good friends. She was one of those skinny, wiry women who thrive on work. Redheaded, too. But I never noticed that her temper was any worse than that of the general run of humanity.

"Hi," she said. "I'm giving them beef stew for supper so I've got a little time to visit."

Richanne ran the cookhouse for the bachelors and most afternoons she was too busy cooking to have any time for visiting. The men got in from the woods about five o'clock and they liked to eat right away because their evenings were so short. Well, they had to get up at four-thirty in order to have breakfast before they went to work so pretty much everyone in camp was in bed by nine or nine-thirty.

7

"Come on in," I invited. "Like some tea?"

Richanne laid her coat over the arm of the couch and sat down at the table.

"Sure."

I put the kettle back on and it only took a minute for the water to boil again. I got the sugar bowl and put it on the table. I don't sweeten my tea but I knew Richanne liked hers with a couple of spoonfuls of sugar.

"What do you know that's new?" I asked, as I dropped a teabag in a cup and draped the string over the rim. I filled the cup with boiling water and set it in front of Richanne.

"Oh, not too much," she said, dipping the teabag up and down until she had the strength she wanted. "I hear Orville Patterson's yelling for Francine Morton's blood."

I was surprised at that. Francine was formerly Mrs. Orville Patterson but had been married to Jim Morton long enough to produce two children, the older one a girl in the midst of the terrible twos.

"What on earth for? They've been divorced about four years now, haven't they?"

"Mmmmmmmmm, not that long. More like three."

"Well, long enough for Orville to get over it, anyway."

8

"You'd think so. But Jim was singing at that dance in Spray last Saturday night and Francine danced a couple of dances with Orville. Right in the middle of the dance floor, he started shouting at her -- that she was a two-timing bitch and Jim was a fool."

"I can't believe Francine danced with him. Or that he asked her. They strike sparks every time they get within screaming distance of each other."

"Well, Jim jumped down off the bandstand right in the middle of a song and decked Orville. Orville left the dance and went on over to Mitchell and sat in the tavern there until it closed. He was telling everyone who'd listen that Francine not only did him wrong but was doing Jim wrong."

"My lord. Did he say who else was involved?"

"Not right out. At least not that I know of. He kind of hinted around that Francine and Mason Sturdevant had something going. But I swear I don't know when they'd have time to do anything."

"It wouldn't be easy, the hours this camp keeps."

Richanne laughed. "Not like in town where there's places to meet. Taverns and restaurants and motels, even. Well, I'd better get on up the road. I want to get the men fed and out of the way early tonight so I can get home before the kids start trick-or-treating."

"They're sure excited. I could hardly keep them in the room after our Halloween party."

"I don't blame them. It's about the only excitement they get, outside of the Christmas program."

Richanne put her cup and saucer and spoon in the sink, rinsing out the cup. "What are you going to treat them with? Give them all A's on their math papers?"

I laughed. "Uh-uh. I picked up some Hershey bars and Mountain bars when I was in Heppner last weekend. Unfortunately, I've eaten most of the Mountain bars. But I'll have enough to go around -- if they don't come twice."

Richanne put on her coat. "I made some popcorn balls and a big batch of chocolate cupcakes."

"They'll have enough candy and treats to keep them sick for a week." I opened the door for Richanne. "Good luck hurrying the men up tonight."

"Oh, they'll hurry up, all right. I'll see to that." Richanne went out and I closed the door and sat down at the table again but couldn't settle down to grading papers. The Jim-Francine-Orville triangle was an ugly mess and had been for several years. In my opinion both men were too good for her but it wasn't my opinion that mattered. Francine was pretty enough but I had never been able to see what there was about her that made otherwise sensible men act like idiots. My own brother had fallen for her at one time. I never did know just how far that went but I know my sister-in-law had a bad six months.

Francine Davis Patterson Morton was a pianist. She was really good, not just the usual good enough to get by player who plays with small bands and combos all over America. She was from somewhere in California originally and had reputedly been on her way to a promising career as a concert pianist when she paid a visit to some relatives in Bend. Orville was living in Bend at the time and they met at an Elks picnic or something. They got married right away and almost immediately things went sour between them. They stuck it out for two or three years, then Francine met Jim.

Jim Morton was a country and western singer, maybe good enough for the big time. I knew he'd done a few talent scout programs on the radio and one on a TV station in Portland a year or so ago. Why he chose to live up here in the backwoods was beyond me. Of course, he was raised in mill towns and had lived in Kinzua as a boy and again when he was married to his first wife. But I didn't see how he expected to launch a singing career from this logging camp. He worked as a cat-skinner on the construction crew so he and Francine had one of the bigger, nicer houses.

I couldn't see why the idea of Francine having an affair should come as such a shock to Jim. After all, she had an affair with him before she left Orville. I suppose he thought it was different with him.

I didn't say so to Richanne but I knew Francine and Mason were making a fool of Jim. Jim can't be on the bandstand singing and watch Francine all the time, too. She refused to demean her art by playing with the local bands. A few weeks ago I had been at a dance in Kinzua with Boyd Atkins when Jim was singing. The hall was overheated and I stepped out onto the porch for some air and happened to see Francine out in the parking lot. When she got to the last row of cars, the door opened and she got in. It might have been innocent, of course, but it wasn't. It was the back door that opened and it was Mason's car. I just went back in to the dance, it wasn't any of my business -- I only wished people wouldn't do such foolish, hurtful things. Because Jim was bound to hear about it sooner or later, that sort of thing can't be kept secret, and I hated to see Jim hurt. He was a nice guy and he and the two kids deserved better.

I put the mess out of my mind and went back to the math quizzes. It was a real challenge to teach four grades with students of wildly differing abilities. Most of them, of course, were by definition average. But the Miller twins had bright, inquisitive minds that ranged practically over the whole body of human endeavor while Cynthia Masour's intelligence was barely dull-normal. Dottie and Debbie Miller were in the fifth grade but they often turned in the assignments for all four grades and did very well, too, even in the eighth grade work. On these particular quizzes, Debbie had scored a hundred percent on the fifth, sixth, and seventh grade quizzes but dropped to ninety-two on the eighth grade quiz. Dottie had scored in the nineties on all four quizzes. Her forte was English.

I put the graded papers aside to take back to school in the morning and set about getting myself some dinner. I often ate with my Aunt Genevieve and Uncle Miles but I knew she would be busy with Halloween treats tonight. Uncle Miles was foreman of the construction crew and Aunt Genevieve was a nurse, which made it nice in times of emergency because the nearest doctor is about thirty miles away. I used to spend my summers with them and my cousins. Phil is a year older than me and was now riding the rodeo circuit, trying to make a living by getting his bones broken. This time of year he would be in Texas or Oklahoma, working as a ranch hand. Lorraine was about a year younger than me -- she was married and lived out near Hardman so I got to see her pretty regularly.

There was some venison steak in the refrigerator so I boiled a potato and opened a can of green beans. I made gravy from the drippings I'd fried the steak in and had quite a nice little dinner. I had just finished and was clearing the table when I heard the first trick-or-treaters coming. Actually, I was sure they could be heard all over camp. There was a lot of shouting and laughing and general hilarity. They were coming down from the bachelor bunkhouses -- the kids always went there first because the unmarried men were so generous. I remember trick-or-treating with my cousins years ago and we'd often get candy and fruit and nickels from each man. I had much preferred to trick-or-treat at Camp Five instead of in town.

A loud banging at the door brought me with a bowl of candy bars. There were five kids, all wearing masks. But they were also wearing their coats so I knew who they were. Not that it mattered. I dropped a Hershey bar into each sack, noticing that they were half full already. It was getting really cold, too, and the snow was coming down heavily. It was about two inches deep by then. The trick-or-treaters thanked me politely and scampered off to the next house. Then a covey of small kids knocked on the door. A couple of mothers hovered in the back and there was a chorus of "twick-or-tweat." I "tweated" them and one of the mothers prompted them to say "thank you," which they did and then trundled off to the next house. There are only twenty-two school-age children in camp, not counting Eileen Chichester, the high school senior. Eileen would be terribly insulted to be counted among the children. With the twenty or so pre-schoolers, it didn't take long for the kids to make their trick-or-treating demands and go home to examine their loot.

Chapter 2

I settled down with a book, Agatha Christie's latest. Poirot was baffled for the nonce while Hastings was making idiotic suggestions and I was enjoying it all a good deal. How exotic and, at the same time, homey and cozy rural England seemed. It was nearly bedtime and I had to make a trip to the bath house that I had put off about as long as practical. I slipped on my coat and galoshes and, picking up my flashlight (the moon being our only street light in Camp Five), went outside. Most of the houses were dark. The flashlight was superfluous as it had stopped snowing, the wind was rising and the clouds were breaking up, allowing enough moonlight to see by.

On the way back I admired the snowscape. There was enough snow to frost the branches of the evergreens and cover the roofs. There's something heart-wrenchingly lovely about a snow scene at night and in the mountains it is at its loveliest. I was almost home when I heard a scream. I stopped dead, paralyzed with the horror of it. It might have been a cougar. Cougars scream at night and the sound is like a woman's scream of terror. I had heard cougars scream several times and I knew that one had been prowling around camp this fall. I had seen its tracks myself in a damp patch at the edge of the playground. Some of the men wanted to hunt it down and kill it but most of us wanted it left alone. It was only curious and would soon tire of civilization and retreat farther into the mountains.

As I stood there, all this running through my mind, the scream came again. I glimpsed movement from the corner of my eye. Someone or something was running between the houses to my right, toward the meadow. The Granvilles' collies were barking and Richanne Worley's cocker spaniel was having hysterics. Vaguely, I wondered why Fritz, Carl Chichester's weimeraner, hadn't joined the chorus. I went slowly and cautiously toward the place where I'd seen the movement, in the shadow of a house and a copse of pine trees. I could see well enough to move around but not well enough to distinguish details in the shadows. I turned my flashlight on and looked for tracks. The ground was well trampled with the children's boots and overshoes and I couldn't see any cat tracks. I stopped and looked around. All at once, I was frightened. Not just scared because of the scream in the night, but personally frightened, as if I were being stalked with deadly intent. As if someone or something was watching me.

I turned off my flashlight and stepped into the shadows cast by the Mortons' house. Trying to look in all directions at once, I hurried back toward my house, past the Mortons' back door. A sound made me whip my head around to look behind. The snow wasn't wet or cold enough to crunch, it was soft and feathery underfoot. The sound had been a sort of swishing noise. Like the movement of cloth against cloth; dress against slip or jacket arms against jacket body. My heart was beating 'way too fast and my breath was 'way too noisy. I shrieked as a man stepped around the corner of the Millers' house and came toward me. As I started to run, I tripped and fell, trying to break my fall with my hands.

Jim Morton stooped over me. It took me a few seconds to recognize him.

"Oh, Jim. Thank God it's you."

"Marge!" A tad of humor peeked through his consternation. "What are you doing? Who did you think I was?"

I wasn't paying any attention to Jim's questions. It had been borne upon me that I had not merely fallen in the snow, I was definitely hurt; I couldn't

18

tell how badly. Jim helped me up and I saw that I had fallen on a porcupine. The porky waddled slowly away. My coat had opened as I fell and my front was dreadfully painful. I knew that I was covered with porcupine quills. It suddenly dawned on Jim, too.

"Oh, my God, Marge, are you full of porky quills? Here, I'll take you home and pull them out."

"You will not!" I was in for an ordeal, I knew, but I wasn't going to have Jim Morton and a pair of pliers working on my naked stomach. The very idea made me bright red with embarrassment. "Walk me home, Jim, that's all I need."

"That's not all you need. You need a good stiff shot of whiskey and a strong hand with a pair of pliers."

We started to walk toward my house. I was surprised how much it hurt to walk. The movement of my clothes against the quills was excruciating. Involuntarily, I whimpered.

"Lucky I happened by," Jim said, probably with the idea of taking my mind off the pain. "I went up to talk to old Mike Novotny. He lives in one of the bunkhouses, you know. I like the old boy."

"I don't think I've ever met him," I said. It may seem strange that in a community of about a hundred people, there would be people who had never met one another. But the bachelors and the families didn't mix much, outside of work.

As I spoke, I saw a form go past the children's swings, moving rapidly down the hill. I lost it in the shadows cast by the houses and couldn't locate it again. I thought it was a man but it might have been a woman. It wasn't a cougar. Jim didn't seem to see it.

"He's a character. He's Czech, you know. Came to this country more than forty years ago but still speaks broken English."

I didn't answer. No matter how much of a character and good old guy, he was, I just couldn't get interested in Mike Novotny right then. We were at my house anyway. I went up the steps with Jim holding my arm.

"Thanks, Jim. I'll be okay now."

"What were you doing prowling around in the dead of night?"

"I thought I saw someone in the shadows and I went to see what was going on."

"You ought to quit being such a nosy little busybody, Marge. What if it had been that cougar instead of a porcupine? You might have been badly mauled or even killed."

"Nonsense. Good night, Jim. Thanks."

"You're sure you won't let me help you get those

quills out? It's not as easy as you might think."

Well, I was tempted. I knew it wasn't going to be easy to take them out myself. I'd seen Uncle Miles take quills out of a dog's muzzle once. It was obviously painful and took quite a long time. But modesty won out and I sent Jim home.

I went over to a kitchen cupboard and took down a bottle of Canadian Club. I poured about an ounce in a glass and tossed it down, shuddering as it slid down my throat. I detest the taste of whiskey, either bourbon or scotch, but I didn't have any vodka or wine. And I didn't think creme de cocoa would be strong enough to do any good under these circumstances. I took three aspirins and tried to wash the whiskey taste out of my mouth with a glass of water. Opening the curtains in front of the sink and leaving the water to drip so the pipes wouldn't freeze, I rummaged in the catch-all drawer for the pliers.

In the bedroom I stripped, whimpering as my movements stirred the quills in my flesh, then slid into my chenille robe and slippers. Although the house was warm, it wasn't warm enough to stand around entirely naked. I swiveled the mirror on the dresser down so I could see the quills -- from my waist to my hips, I was almost as thickly covered with quills as the porcupine had been. There was a

21

bottle of isopropyl alcohol in one of the kitchen cupboards. I went and got it and a piece of waxed paper to lay on top of the dresser and went to work.

That was easily the worst hour of my life to date. Some of the quills were only lightly stuck into my skin but many of them were driven in deeply and were hard to pull out. Porcupine quills are barbed. Not with one big barb but with scores, maybe hundreds, of tiny barbs that keep the quills in and work them deeper, if they aren't pulled out right away. I don't think the quills knew anything about the aspirin or the Canadian Club, either. I'd worked on them for maybe ten minutes when I went back for another shot. I figured if it didn't ease the pain, it would eventually fix it so I wouldn't give a damn. So I made it a double and went back to work on the quills.

I got them all out eventually and washed off the blood. I was sore and lonesome and slightly drunk. I put on a flannel nightie and crawled into bed, lying on my side, not wanting to even think about the weight of the blankets on my stomach. I slept only fitfully. About midnight there was a noise just outside my house. I was instantly wide awake but the wind was still blowing and whatever the noise was, it was muffled so I couldn't identify it. I was trying to think what it might be: A deer bumping

22

into my garbage can; a limb breaking off one of the big ponderosa pines; a man tripping over my chopping block and falling? I got up and looked out the window. The bedroom window was high and small and all I could see was that it was snowing again.

The big feathery flakes were piling up quickly. If it kept on, we would have six or eight inches by morning. As I stood watching the storm, I thought I heard a car start somewhere down near the old road to Kinzua. The road wasn't maintained anymore but it was still passable, with care, even in the snow. It was cold and I got back into bed, pulling the covers up snugly around my neck.

At five o'clock I heard the crummies start in front of the foremen's houses. The vehicles that carried the men out to the woods were called crummies, I suppose because they always seemed to be battered and worn and on their last go-round. Ralph Buies would have the little road grader we called the grasshopper out plowing the road between camp and Kinzua and then out to the woods toward the highway to Heppner. I was glad to stay in bed, cozy, if not comfy, and drift back to sleep. When I woke again it was eight o'clock, time to get up and face the day.

My stomach was sore and covered with puncture

wounds and bruises. I knew I should dab iodine or mercurochrome on the holes but I couldn't bring myself to touch them. I took some more aspirin and brushed my teeth, trying to get the taste of whiskey out once and for all. Besides, it would never do to show up at school with whiskey on my breath. Hopefully, the kids wouldn't notice that I had a bit of a hangover. I pulled my galoshes on over my slippers and buttoned my coat over my nightgown. I caught up a towel and opened the door. It was still snowing but the wind had died down to almost nothing. It was cold but not bitterly so as I walked over to the bath house. There were a few fresh tracks in the snow which was about five inches deep where the wind hadn't either blown it away or piled it up in drifts.

Omega Price was washing her hands when I went into the bath house.

"Good morning, Marge."

"Good morning." I hurried into a stall, hoping Omega wasn't feeling chatty. I like Omega all right but, my goodness, she's a talker.

"Heard the news?"

The sound of the water running stopped and I knew she had a budget of some kind of news that she was eager to share.

"News?" I asked. "In Camp Five? You're

24

kidding, of course."

"'Fraid not. Francine Morton ran away last night."

When I came out of the stall, Omega was leaned up against one of the sinks, as if she had all day to gossip, which I guess she did since her husband would be gone until about five in the afternoon. She and Cleve had no children and it doesn't take long to do the work in a two-room house. I turned the water on but it takes slightly less than forever to get the water hot so I splashed cold water on my face.

"Ran away? With whom?"

"I'm not sure. All I know is Jim asked Twyla Schuyler to babysit today while he went to work."

I dried my face and hands.

"Maybe Francine is sick."

"Nope. She's gone."

I stared at Omega. Omega grinned at me.

"Yep. Jim told Kathy Schuyler that Francine left last night and asked her if Twyla could take care of the girls today. He's called his mother, or rather had Mrs. Hamilton call her, and she's going to come up today but she can't get here before tonight, of course. She lives somewhere over by Lakeview. Plush or Adel or one of those places, doesn't she?"

"I don't know. I never heard where Jim's mother lives."

"Well, anyway, it'll take all day for her to get here. I'm surprised that Jim didn't leave Danny with the girls and save the cost of a baby-sitter."

That surprised me, too. Not that Jim would begrudge the cost of a baby-sitter but I knew Danny adored his little half-sisters and was very good with them. Danny was Jim's son by an earlier marriage and had just come to live with his father at the beginning of this school year. He was a sophomore at Wheeler County High in Fossil so I didn't know him very well, never having spent any time with him. I'd just seen him around camp and heard what other people thought of him. In spite of the fact that he hadn't lived in Kinzua since he was a small boy and had been raised mostly in Ashland, he'd taken to life in the logging camp and seemed to fit right in.

"Maybe there's something special going on at school that Jim didn't think Danny should miss," I said. It didn't sound very likely to me, even as I said it, and I could see that Omega didn't think much of it, either.

"Maybe. Well, I left a cherry pie in the oven, I'd better see how it's doing."

Omega left and I followed her out into the snow. It was coming down steadily, as if it meant to snow for a long time. I knew the kids would be excited and delighted.

I made some coffee and while it perked on the stove, I got out the ingredients for pancakes. But I wasn't in the mood for pancakes so I put the eggs and milk back in the fridge and made myself a couple of slices of toast. Aunt Genevieve had given me a jar of huckleberry jam and I spread a thick layer on the toast. Wonderful. Either the coffee or the aspirin had eased my headache enough to just about forget about it but the whole front of my body stung. I dressed and straightened things up, grimacing as I washed the pliers and put them back in the catch-all drawer. Maybe I'd stop in and ask Aunt Genevieve to put something on those puncture wounds after school this afternoon.

Walking to school was so beautiful that I wished there was a long way around so I could take it. The snow looked soft and fluffy as it fell and as it blanketed the world. The morning light was pearly, casting a gracious radiance on everything in sight. The air was cold and crisp, inducing brisk movement, so that the feelings roused by the sense of touch were in sharp contrast to the feelings produced by the sense of sight. Somehow the combination was exciting and made me feel positively euphoric, in spite of my sore stomach and slight hangover.

Many of the children were already on their way

to school. They were affected in much the same way I was by the weather -- they were laughing and calling back and forth. A good many snowballs were flying to and fro.

Debbie and Dottie Miller came past me, walking quickly. I told them good morning and received a burst of gibberish back, accompanied by grins and waves. The twins had lately invented a language and had been very trying with it. They took spells of speaking nothing but "Quoskeen," as they called it, much to the irritation of their peers. I had no doubt that their language possessed a full set of grammatical rules and standardized spelling -- the twins were very bright and thorough -- but English was the language I was supposed to be teaching them. I had suggested to their parents that they buy the girls some of those phonograph records that teach foreign languages, French or Italian or even Russian, but they said the girls weren't interested in any foreign language but their own. The Millers didn't see any harm in the girls' inventing a language and I didn't either, really, except that I felt the time and energy might have been used for more practical purposes. Paul Miller pointed out that they might have been used for many more detrimental purposes, which I had to admit was true.

Lyle Allston and Mason Troupe were waiting for

me to unlock the door so they could get the flag and run it up. At precisely 8:45 Cynthia Masour presented herself at my desk and asked for the whistle, it being her week for calling the upper grades inside. I usually had to remind whoever was supposed to do it but Cynthia was always punctual. The kids came in, rosy-cheeked and shining-eyed from the cold and snow. We said the "Pledge of Allegiance" and they sat down and looked at me expectantly. I handed out the arithmetic assignments to the fifth, seventh, and eighth grades, then called the sixth grade up to the board. Ray Troupe and Bobby Cabusap were quite reasonably bright and quick but Doreen Cranston was a different kettle of fish. Besides which, arithmetic was definitely not her subject. We delved into the intricacies of fractions and my attention was pretty much fully engaged. I wish I could say the same for Doreen's. Out of the corner of my eye I noticed that Dottie and Debbie were whispering and writing in a way that seemed to have nothing to do with arithmetic.

As soon as I finished with the sixth grade, I collected the arithmetic papers from the other classes. Dottie and Debbie handed in completed papers and I sighed. I felt it would take a full-time tutor to make the twins use their minds to capacity. I put the fifth, sixth, and seventh grades to work on

29

English compositions, giving the Miller girls the subject, "Weather Patterns in the Western United States." That ought to hold them for a day or two. The problem was, there weren't many reference books in our tiny library. In fact, there weren't many books at all. But I knew they had an Encyclopedia Britannica at home and there were a couple of science books in the school library that would help. Plus, I would be going into Kinzua that evening and I could bring back books from the school library there. Not that there were many in that library, either, but there ought to be something helpful.

Having settled down three grades with writing assignments, I went to give Mason Troupe a lesson in diagramming sentences. With Twyla out, baby-sitting for Jim Morton, I could give Mason some individual attention, which he needed. Twyla had caught onto diagramming pretty quickly but Mason couldn't seem to get the hang of it. At the end of half-an-hour of specialized instruction, I wasn't sure he was ever going to get the hang of it. He said he didn't see what the use of it was and my explanation that it would give him a better grasp of the language and how to use it effectively didn't seem to convince him.

It was the custom to read aloud to the kids after lunch for fifteen minutes or so. It wasn't always easy to find a book that all four grades could relate to; there's a big difference in the interests of ten-year-olds and thirteen-year-olds. But luckily I'd struck pay dirt with a book about pioneer days up around Pendleton. It was close enough geographically that the kids could easily identify with the characters' way of life and tribulations yet far enough technologically that they could wonder at the absence of running water in the houses and no electricity and only horses for transportation. To tell the truth, I was enjoying it as much as they were and when they groaned as I was about to stop in an exciting place, our time for storybooks having run out, I weakened and continued for a few minutes to see how the episode came out. I am happy to tell you that the bear did *not* attack the little pioneer girl nor her father, whose only weapon was a Bowie knife, but only tore their wagon apart searching for food.

Chapter 3

The afternoon slipped along at a tolerably quick speed. My many tiny wounds were still painful and the least pressure on my abdomen was misery. I decided that I would have to see Aunt Genevieve right after school. I hadn't had a chance to talk to Sylvia Ziegler all day. Morning recess usually coincided for all eight grades and we would chat while the kids played. Today, we had kept the children in and had recess in the gym, the first through fourth grades had gone at 10:00 and the fifth through eighth at 10:15. I suggested "Red Rover" as being sufficiently rowdy without being injurious and the children had chosen up sides and run at one another with lots of shouting and hollering.

Sylvia dismissed her four grades at the same time I called afternoon recess for mine so we generally chatted then, too. I was out on the playground, watching the boys organize themselves into two armies so they could pelt one another with snowballs -- I knew the armies would soon unite in order to declare war on the girls and pelt them instead -- when Sylvia opened the door and the little ones poured outside. She helped with some galoshes and mittens and buttoned Delphine Granville's pretty blue coat. Delphine was six, blue-eyed and golden-haired and just as pretty as a child could possibly be. Having gotten her crew squared away and on their way home, Sylvia came over to talk. It had snowed all day and was still snowing but the wind had died down. The snow was about ten inches deep by then.

"Hi," I greeted her.

"Hi," she smiled. "How about this snow, so early in the year?"

"I don't mind. I like snow."

"I thought you were going to Kinzua this afternoon?"

"I am. They'll have the road plowed."

Sylvia grimaced. "Sooner you than me. I'd hate to meet one of those big Kenworths in the snow."

"They should have made their last haul for the day by the time I start."

"I'd think you'd want to go as early as you could so you could get back before dark."

"I have to stop by Aunt Genevieve's first."

Sylvia is too polite to ask personal questions

33

directly but her facial expression was one big interrogation point. I thought about telling her about the porcupine but decided not to.

"Can I get anything for you in Kinzua?"

"No, I don't think so. Max and I went in day before yesterday for Halloween candy and groceries."

"I've got to stop at the school library and get some books. I assigned some composition themes that will require a little research."

"It's a shame we have so few books available. And what we do have are mostly outdated."

"Fortunately, the kids don't know that. Even our songbooks were published about the turn of the century. I think the latest ditty in them is "Come away with Me, Lucille, in My Merry Oldsmobile.""

Sylvia laughed. "Oh, well, those old songs are good for group singing."

Just then Darla Ziegler, Cynthia Masour, and the Miller twins came running up, trying to shelter behind us as the boys, true to form, chased them with snowballs. Dottie got a face full of snow and Debbie turned on the boys furiously, letting loose a stream of gibberish that sounded distinctly as though it should be spelled with asterisks, pound signs, and ampersands. Dottie wiped the snow off her face and also began to berate the boys in

"Quoskeen."

"Aw," broke in Ray Troupe, "talk English. You know we can't understand that stupid bunk."

Dottie replied, though not in English. Ray stooped and scooped up a wad of snow as big as a basketball and rammed it into Debbie's face. Dottie immediately let out a screech and began to pound him with her fists. I waded in to separate them and my poor stomach got jabbed in the general melee but I pulled them apart and finally got Dottie to stop hitting.

In the meantime, Lyle Allston had got into the act somehow and Debbie took off chasing him. He looked over his shoulder to shout, "Nyah, nyah, nyah," at her derisively, and ran right into a hole alongside the schoolgrounds, near the Morton house. Jim had started to dig a hole for some purpose or other. It was about two feet in diameter and I didn't know how deep. Didn't know until Lyle fell into it, that is. Jim had covered it with a canvas tarp weighted around the edge with rocks but, of course, the rocks weren't enough to hold the tarp in place when a husky seventh-grader fell on it. We all rushed over to see if he was hurt and to help him out. He stood up, laughing, and I could see the hole was about three feet deep. Mason and Ray hauled him out and they pulled the tarp back into place and put the rocks back where they belonged.

I sent the kids inside and Sylvia waved goodbye as she went along home. The afternoon was relatively quiet. I'm glad to say that Doreen now knows that the Nile River is in Egypt and that it flows south to north. Geography definitely isn't Doreen's best subject. Ray and Bobby, the other two sixth graders, are much quicker in most subjects, although Doreen can far outdistance either of them in any track event. Her batting average is a lot better than theirs, too.

After school I walked over to Aunt Genevieve's. It was still snowing and looked as if it would snow forever. I found Aunt Genevieve industriously knitting. She makes the most amazingly beautiful sweaters. This one was mint green and white, made of some kind of very fine, silky wool. Being left-handed, I had never succeeded in learning to knit or crochet. I find that even when I'm doing it right, it looks wrong to my right-handed teachers, and merely makes everyone frustrated. So I gave up trying to learn.

"Hi, Aunt Genevieve."

She looked up and smiled at me. Aunt Genevieve is a truly beautiful woman. She is plump and her eyes are the loveliest clear, deep blue. Like the blue of Crater Lake. But her greatest beauty is of personality and character. When Uncle Miles, who was my dad's younger brother, wanted to go into the Seabees during the war, Aunt Genevieve moved to Heppner, got a job with Doc Haynes, and sent him off with a smile. I know it was hard, working and raising Phil and Lorraine by herself and worrying about Uncle Miles when all the news from the Pacific was so bad for so long. But Aunt Genevieve never complained, never faltered. She is some punkins, is Aunt Genevieve.

"Hi, Marge. Is it three-thirty, already?"

"Sure is." I sat down in Uncle Miles' chair and leaned back, luxuriating in the soft comfort of the best chair I've ever sat in.

"There are some Toll House Cookies, if you'd like some."

"No, thanks. I'm kind of in a hurry. I've got to run into Kinzua yet this afternoon. Is there anything you need?"

Aunt Genevieve glanced out the window and frowned at me. "In this snow? It's pretty bad out there. Can't it wait a day or two?"

"I guess it could but it's not storming badly now and it may later on. I'd rather go now and be done with it. Besides, I assigned the Miller twins a report that they need books from the Kinzua school library for."

"Well, if you're set on going, you might pick up some eating apples for me, if they've got any in the store. I've got a craving for apples."

"What kind? Red Delicious?"

"If they've got them. Or Jonathan. Any kind of sweet apple."

"Okay. Aunt Genevieve, I had an accident last night and fell on a porcupine."

Aunt Genevieve let her hands drop to her lap. "Why didn't you come right over?"

"It was kind of late. I pulled the quills out all right but I couldn't bring myself to put iodine on the holes. Would you do it for me?"

Before I even got all that said, Aunt Genevieve was on her feet, her knitting forgotten. "Come right in here and let me look," she ordered.

I followed her into the bathroom and pulled off my dress while she took the iodine bottle out of the medicine chest. When she turned around and saw the puncture marks all over my middle she shook her head commiseratingly. Gently, she pulled down the elastic of my panties and half-slip.

"Heavens above, Margie," she said.

"It looks worse than it is, but it is sore," I told her.

"I'm going to put some peroxide on those punctures."

I stretched out on Lorraine's bed and Aunt Genevieve gently dabbed hydrogen peroxide on all the little holes. She scolded me a little when some of them fizzed a bit, then she touched each one with iodine. It stung like fury and if I didn't look like something when she was finished! But I felt better with the fear of infection gone.

When I was dressed again, I put my coat on and Aunt Genevieve followed me out to the back porch. I put my galoshes on.

"You come back tomorrow after school and let me see those wounds again," she said.

"Okay. I'll see you tonight when I bring the apples."

"Be careful driving, now. That road can be treacherous, you know."

"I know. I'll be careful."

I gave her a quick kiss on the cheek and went out the back door.

My Pontiac started with the first flick of the key. It's several years old – Dad gave it to me when I graduated from high school -- but it's never given me any trouble. Not so much as a flat tire, knock on wood. While it warmed up, I got the broom and swept the snow off the hood and windows. It got a little exciting getting out of camp. The street leading up to the road is steep and kind of narrow. My rear wheels spun and I fought to correct without overcorrecting. I have never really understood that bit about how you're supposed to steer in the direction of the skid in order to pull out of the skid. I mean, that just puts you in the ditch. So I did my usual steer with the skid, steer away from the skid, back and forth while exerting just the right amount of pressure on the accelerator to keep forward momentum without pouring too much power into the skid. Driving on slippery roads was a nightmare for me but I always managed to keep it in the road; sometimes just by the skin of my teeth. This time the tires caught hold and I made it up to the road slipping and sliding only a little. The snow was still coming down in big soft lazy flakes that were very beautiful to watch. My headlights weren't any help in showing me the road but they would at least warn any other travelers that I was there. Aside from meeting the grasshopper on its return from the Kinzua end of the road, I didn't meet anyone.

The lights of Kinzua kind of sprang up all at once, at close quarters. You came around a big curve and there it was, looking as if it had grown on the hills instead of being manmade. It was old as towns go in Oregon and all the buildings were of board and bat, the same as Camp Five. "Downtown" consisted of half a dozen businesses. The company store occupied the first floor of the biggest building, which was also the tallest at three stories. It featured groceries, clothing, household goods, hardware, and notions; a hotel of sorts was above the store for single people who didn't rate a whole house, unmarried school teachers and office workers and such; the beauty shop was also in the store building. The post office was a little building beside the store. Across the street there was a Texaco service station and the building that housed the pastime, the confectionery, and the barber shop. There was a golf course out of town a mile or so and a rough landing strip for the owners when they flew their Cessna in on their infrequent inspection tours.

The road from Camp Five forked at the log pond, one fork going through the mill yard and up the hill to the business section, the other fork going up the hill to the school. I went to the school first, knowing I'd have to catch Julie Staverton, the janitor, to let me into the library before she finished for the day. Luckily she was in the hall near the front door when I went up the steps. I rapped on the window and she jumped as if I'd poked her with a cattle prod. Patting her chest, she came to the door and opened it.

"For heaven's sake, Marge, you scared me half to death. Here I was, thinking about getting home to

41

cook supper for Les and the boys, and here comes a knock like the sound of doom. I had no idea anyone else was anywhere near this school."

"I'm sorry, Julie." I stepped into the hall and closed the door. "I didn't mean to startle you. I just need to get some books from the library."

"Go ahead, take what you want. Only don't forget to leave the cards so Mrs. Morris will know where the books have gone."

"Thanks. I won't be long."

"Good. I'm about ready to lock up."

I went down the hall to the tiny library and Julie went back to pushing her thirty-six-inch dustmop. The library was organized according to the Dewey Decimal System but it wasn't really necessary. There were so few books that it only took a few minutes to see what was available on scientific subjects. There wasn't anything directly relating to weather, or at least only relating to weather, but I picked up a couple of books that had some weather incorporated into broad categories of geography. I found a few other books that would be useful in the next couple of weeks and signed the cards and left them under a paperweight on the librarian's desk.

Julie was putting her dustmop in the broom closet when I went out into the hall.

"Okay, Julie, I'm finished. You need a ride down

the hill?"

"No, thanks. I'd rather walk. It's only a little ways and walking isn't anywhere near as scary as riding in a car on that hill in the snow."

I laughed and thought ruefully that she was certainly right about that. "Yes, indeed. I'll see you, then. Be careful, it's pretty slippery."

Julie opened the door and I stepped out onto the porch. "You be careful, too. Especially going back to camp."

"I will."

I left Julie putting on her overshoes and got into my car. I got down the hill to the store without any major skids and picked up some apples for Aunt Genevieve and a few other things I needed, then headed back home. It was just about mile post one that my lights picked up a figure walking along the side of the road. It turned to flag me down and I saw that it was Danny Morton. Naturally, I stopped. There are no strangers in the mountains (except during hunting season, when all the would-be great hunters in the cities come out to make fools of themselves) and custom demands that we stop and give our neighbors a lift. Danny normally rode the school bus to the high school in Fossil and back so I was surprised to see him there. He opened the door and brushed the snow off his coat and knocked the snow off his boots as he got in, giving me a smile that looked rather forced.

"Hi, Danny. Nice weather we're having."

"Yeah. Thanks for picking me up."

"Glad to do it. Pretty cold night for an eleven-mile walk."

"Sure is. I missed the bus."

"From Fossil?" As soon as I asked it, I knew it was a dumb question. There hadn't been near enough time to walk the twenty miles between Fossil and Kinzua since the final period of the day.

Danny shot me a look as if he were revising his estimate of my intelligence. "No. I had an errand in Kinzua and I couldn't ask Mrs. Cranston to wait for me."

Virginia Cranston used her Ford station wagon to take the four high schoolers from Camp Five to Kinzua, where they caught the bus in front of the company store and rode with the Kinzua high school students to Fossil. In the afternoons, she met them there for the trip back to camp. I don't know why she took the job, she didn't really need the money; her husband was a timber-faller. She was an awful old crab and had no patience at all with the kids. It wouldn't have hurt her to wait a few minutes if one of the kids needed to run into the store to pick something up. But she never would. She wouldn't

44

accept little commissions from her neighbors, either, so anyone who needed something our little store couldn't supply would have to drive clear into Kinzua for it. That was maybe a little more understandable. It could have turned into a full-time job doing people's shopping for them.

Danny stared straight ahead into the dazzling whiteness of the snowflakes falling through the beams of my headlights. I flicked a quick look at him and he seemed preoccupied. I was puzzled because he'd always before seemed like a cheerful kid. I was quite startled when I spoke to him and he jumped as if he'd heard a voice in a supposedly empty haunted house. He made a visible effort to seem natural.

"I'm sorry, what did you say?"

I grinned at him. "I just asked how you liked school by now."

"It's okay. I'd like to go out for football but Dad says he can't pick me up after practice every night. I could hitchhike home, there's always someone coming back to camp about the time the bus drops off the guys in Kinzua. But Dad won't let me."

"That's too bad. I know the Falcons need every man they can get."

"Yeah. We've got 107 students this year so we have to play eleven-man football. We've only got

45

twelve guys out and one of them's Raleigh Stipes. Raleigh's a freshman and weighs about eighty pounds."

"Did you play football last year?"

"Yeah. In Ashland. That's where I lived before. I played half-back on the JV squad. Coach played me quite a bit. I'm pretty good."

We talked football for awhile and then lapsed into silence. Danny fell back into his preoccupied stare. I didn't want to gossip about his step-mother but I did want to know what was going on. Curiosity got the better of scruples, as it so often does.

"I understand your step-mother disappeared last night."

Danny jumped again. "What do you mean disappeared? She didn't disappear, she left. She took off with someone."

I was surprised at the heat in his manner. He seemed angry, whether at Francine for leaving or me for questioning him, I wasn't sure. Teenage boys can be so very volatile.

"I'm sorry, Danny. I didn't mean anything particular. I just heard your grandmother was coming up to take care of things while she's gone."

Danny relaxed a little but he seemed to be on guard as he answered. "Yeah. Dad called Mrs.

Hamilton from the office and she called Grandma. He was going to Heppner to pick her up after work. They ought to be there when I get home."

"She's not driving, then?"

"No. She doesn't like driving, especially in snow. Dad thought Uncle Mark would drive her to Heppner."

"I see. How long is Francine going to be gone?"

To my intense surprise and consternation, Danny turned on me furiously. "I don't know how long she's going to be gone. She may be back tomorrow or next week or never. I don't know and I don't care. What is this quiz, anyway? You're as bad as Mrs. Price."

I was too astonished to answer at first. His shot about Omega Price certainly went home, since it was Omega who had told me about Francine's departure that morning. Danny sat sullenly staring out the side window. I didn't say anything for the simple reason that I couldn't think of anything to say. I didn't want to come across as a prissy school teacher and I didn't know him well enough to pat his shoulder in silent understanding. Besides, which, I didn't understand.

I made the turn off the main road to go down the hill to camp and immediately slid to the shoulder just where the drop was steepest and highest. I'd thought I had slowed enough to make the turn easily but evidently I was more upset that I had realized. I wrenched the steering wheel to the left and accelerated the merest bit. That took the car away from the precipice and swung it ninety degrees so it was crossways in the road with the hood pointed at the embankment. I kept the wheel cramped to the left and hit the brake, hard. We slipped and slid and came to a stop with Chief Pontiac's head out on the hood pointing up the way we'd come.

"Well, hell." I was frightened and shaky and angry. I put my foot on the accelerator but the back tires merely spun ineffectually. "Oh, crap! What the hell am I supposed to do now?"

The question was meant to be rhetorical but Danny answered, sounding amused. "Why don't you back down the hill?"

I looked at him doubtfully then realized that it was the most sensible thing to do. "Good idea," I said and put the lever in reverse position. I gave it a little gas but we didn't start back right away. Spinning the wheels had dug us in so that there was a bit of a snow bank behind the rear wheels. My mind was working again so I moved the gear selector from reverse to drive and back a couple of times, rocking the car so she could climb over the miniature snow banks. I backed down the hill rather erratically -- I knew the men would laugh when they saw my tracks if they weren't snowed over first -- and into the Ziegler's driveway, the first one I came to. I put the car in drive and drove forward down the lower street to drop Danny off.

"Goodnight, Miss O'Connor," he said. "I'm sorry I said what I did." He grinned and added, "I didn't know school teachers could cuss like that."

"Oh. I'm sorry." I was embarrassed. I was supposed to be setting a good example.

I brought the car to a stop and Danny hopped out.

"That's okay. Thanks for the ride."

Before I could answer, he closed the car door and was almost instantly lost to view in the falling snow.

Chapter 4

There was no garage attached to my little house so I parked next to it and went inside with my groceries. The books I left in the car; they would be all right there until morning. I put my perishables in the fridge and took the bag of apples over to Aunt Genevieve. She and Uncle Miles had finished dinner but she offered to fix something for me. I declined but accepted a cup of tea. Aunt Genevieve went out to the kitchen to put the kettle on and I took my coat off and sat down on the couch.

Uncle Miles scowled at me. He was a big man -- a brown-eyed handsome man, in spite of all the gray in the fringe that encircled his baldness. "What's all this about you falling on a porkypine last night?"

I knew his scowl wasn't really for me but was a reflection of his concern for my well-being. I smiled at him affectionately. "Well, I did. That's all."

He snorted. "That isn't all. You got a tummy full of quills, is what Genevieve said. Hurt like hell, didn't it?"

"Sure did. They ought to put bells around their necks and warn people where they are."

Uncle Miles laughed. "You pulled 'em out yourself, huh?"

"Well, it was the middle of the night and I didn't want to bother you or Aunt Genevieve."

"It wouldn't have been a bother -- you ought to know better than that. Next time you need anything, middle of the night or not, you come to us. Anyway, what were you doing out gallivanting around in the middle of the night? On a school night, too."

"It was Halloween, you know. Maybe I was trick or treating."

"More likely you were up to some kind of witchery."

I laughed. "I had gone over to the bath house and I heard a couple of screams and thought I'd check it out."

"I heard those. It was a cougar, honey. Got all the dogs in camp barking, too. Kept me awake until they settled down again. Anyway, cougar or not, you had no business to go running out to see about it. What were you going to do if you found someone in trouble?"

Aunt Genevieve brought me a cup of tea and I thanked her. She brought one for Uncle Miles, too, but he waved it away and she sat down in her chair by the oil stove and sipped it herself. It was deliciously hot and comforting after that entry of mine into camp a few minutes before. The fear of imminent death does leave one somewhat shaken.

"Well," demanded Uncle Miles, "what did you think you could do about it if there was someone screaming?"

"I don't know," I confessed. "I didn't really think that far ahead. I just thought I'd better find out if someone was screaming and if so, why."

He shook his head disgustedly. "Women. Next time you feel like rescuing someone, you'd better come get me or one of the other men. Someone who could actually do something to help."

He picked up his Luckies and Zippo from the end table beside his chair and lit a cigarette.

"Uncle Miles. I know women aren't as strong as men but we're not as helpless and weak as you like to think we are. Why, remember the time the Cranstons' house caught fire last winter when all the men were out in the woods at work? It was the women who put out the fire, wasn't it?"

"Well, it was a woman who started it. Virginia filled her trash burner up with too much paper and kindling and set the chimney afire."

"That's not the point, Uncle Miles. The point is the women put the fire out without any help from the men."

"Now, now, now." Aunt Genevieve never could bear quarrelling of any kind. "Don't get excited, you two. Your uncle is right, Margie, you ought not to go traipsing around in the middle of the night looking for trouble. If you really think there's trouble, you come get him."

I smiled at them both and finished my tea. "All right, I will." I put my coat back on and picked up my empty cup and saucer. "But don't blame me if you lose a lot of sleep, Uncle Miles. Remember you wished it on yourself."

I stooped to kiss the top of his head as I went out to the kitchen and he grinned up at me before he scowled again. "Now don't you torment me, you little vixen. You behave yourself."

Aunt Genevieve followed me out onto the back porch where I'd left my overshoes.

"How are the puncture wounds, Margie? Maybe you'd better come in and let me take a look at them."

I pulled my galoshes on over my shoes. "I'm fine, Aunt Genevieve. Just a little sore. I'll look carefully when I go to bed and if there's the slightest sign of infection, I'll come over before I go to school. Okay?"

She smiled happily and patted my arm. "That's fine, Margie. Would you like some cookies for a bedtime snack? I baked some pecan bars this afternoon."

I kissed her on the cheek and smiled at her. "No, thanks. I've eaten enough Halloween candy to keep me sweet for weeks. Goodnight, Auntie."

I slipped out the back door, closing it quickly to keep the heat inside the house.

It was 'way past my dinner time when I got home and I was ravenous. But I was tired, too, and didn't want to bother about cooking. I opened a can of cream of chicken soup and a jar of the Elberta peaches I'd put up the summer before. While the soup was heating, I built a fire in the trash burner so I'd have hot water. With the addition of a cup of tea and some oyster crackers, I had a fine little supper. I did the dishes and tried to read but I couldn't settle down someway. I was restless and uneasy. I kept thinking about how Danny had reacted to my questions in the car on the way back from Kinzua. The boy was definitely nervous and upset about something connected to his step-mother's disappearance.

I bundled up for a trip to the bath house. As soon as I opened the door, I knew the temperature was dropping. The snow was changing from big, feathery flakes to small crystals that stung when the wind drove them into my face and legs. I closed the door and lowered my head, going as quickly as I could across the open space to the bath house.

Before I opened the door of the bath house for the return trip, I braced myself for the onslaught of the storm. I wondered if Jim and his mother had managed to get home before conditions worsened. I looked over towards the Mortons' but visibility was too poor to see even if there were lights on. I knew I wouldn't sleep until I knew whether Danny needed any help with his little sisters. After all, one was a toddler and the other a six-month-old baby.

I lowered my head to protect my face against the stinging crystals, glancing up from time to time to get my bearings. When I got to the back door, I was so astonished that I nearly fell. The snow had been cleared from the steps and the area all around the bottom step, except for a light dusting made by the falling snow. I had just a moment to notice that there were broad reddish patches showing through when Danny loomed up, carrying a bucket.

"Danny," I gasped, the wind jerking the word out of my mouth. "What on earth --"

"What do you want?" the boy asked, raising his voice over the wind. "What are you doing here?"

He looked both scared and defiant and I was at a loss how to answer for a moment. He must have realized that I was too surprised to be coherent because he set his bucket down and led the way up the steps. He opened the door and motioned me inside. I went, grateful to get in out of that dreadful wind.

"I just wondered if your dad and grandmother got here before the storm got so much worse."

"No. Not yet. They may have to stay in Heppner tonight."

"Do you need anything? Any help with the girls?"

"They're okay. I gave Holly scrambled eggs and toast for supper and gave Misty her bottle. They're both asleep now."

"Okay. I just wanted to make sure you're all right. If you need anything, let me know."

"I will. Are you going to be okay? Do you want me to walk you home?"

I smiled at him. "I'm fine, Danny. Goodnight."

He held the door open for me. "Goodnight, Miss O'Connor."

I went back home, the wind tearing at my breath, the ice crystals beating on my face and legs. As soon as I got inside I put the kettle on. I splashed warm water on my face and when it felt thawed, I got my electric heating pad and curled up on the couch with it on my legs. Wrapped up in my afghan, sipping a cup of rich hot chocolate, I began to shiver but it wasn't long before I was warm clear through. There were some papers I should have graded but I was too sleepy to care.

I woke several times during the night and the storm was howling every time. It was good to cuddle down under my blankets and the thick quilt Grandma Straversky had made when she was a young housewife. When I woke at seven and peeked out to see what the day promised, the wind had died down completely and the snow was falling in tight little crystals.

It was cold enough that my breath made a trailing cloud as I walked to school. I'd started a few minutes early so I could stop at Mortons' and see if Danny was okay for the day. I'd seen Virginia Cranston's station wagon start off to Kinzua but I hadn't seen the kids getting in so I didn't know if Danny had gone to school or not. I went up the back steps and knocked on the door. An elderly woman answered it, holding the baby against her shoulder. She was pink-cheeked and white-haired, the living image of a wholesome, dedicated grandmother. Jim must have taken after his father, I couldn't see that he favored his mother at all. She beckoned me in and stepped back to keep the baby out of the draft when I opened the door.

"Hi, I'm Marge O'Connor. I'm a friend of Jim

and Francine's. I just stopped to see if Danny needed anything."

"Hello, Miss O'Connor. I'm Jim's mother. Danny went to school. Come in and have a cup of coffee."

"I'm so glad to meet you, Mrs. Morton. I can't stay, I'm on my way to school myself. I teach the upper grades here."

Mrs. Morton reared her head back to look at the baby. Apparently satisfied with what she saw, she relaxed and began to pat the baby's back. "Danny said you gave him a ride home from Kinzua last night. Thank you."

"Oh, that was nothing. I was glad to do it. Well, I'd better go on to school. Let me know if you need anything. I live in that little house just up the hill, across from the women's bath house. Anyone can show you."

"Well, thanks, Miss O'Connor. That's nice of you. But I expect we'll be all right."

I had remained right by the back door so as not to track snow all over the kitchen. I opened the door and stepped back outside. The steps and ground were covered with a thin blanket of snow and I could see no sign of the reddish stains I'd seen the night before. Perhaps I'd imagined them. My imagination was always quite vivid. There was a sort of trail of beaten snow covered by the ice crystals of the latter phase of the storm that led around the corner of the house toward the garbage can. I was puzzled but could think of no reason for Danny to beat a path to the garbage can in the middle of a terrific storm. I shrugged and continued on to school.

The children were excitable and hard to keep focused on their various tasks. Debbie and Dottie whispered in Quoskeen until I felt like braining them. Darla Ziegler and Twyla Schuyler giggled together and passed notes while Lyle Allston and Mason Troupe threw spitballs at each other and everyone else. I was much gladder when morning recess came than any of the children.

Sylvia and I forgathered on the playground while the kids frolicked in the snow. Some tried to build a snowman but the snow had a crust of ice on top and was too dry underneath. It was too crusty and dry to make good snowballs, too, which was appreciated by Sylvia and me, if by no one else. So the boys chased the girls and put snow down their necks while the girls shrieked and screamed and a good time was had by all.

Sylvia was standing beside the swings and I joined her there. She had a budget of rumors to broadcast concerning the disappearance of Francine Morton.

"Good morning, Marge." Sylvia was well wrapped up, with a woolen scarf and fur-lined gloves.

"Good morning, Sylvia. Isn't it a glorious day?"

The sun was shining brightly but in an aloof, remote sort of way -- there was no warmth in its rays that morning. But the world was very lovely with the smooth, glittering whiteness that covered everything. The air was still and crisp and the sky was a clear, pure blue with not a cloud in sight.

"Have you heard the latest about Francine Morton?"

"No, is there news? I stopped there on my way to school to see if Jim's mom was there yet. I was there last night to see if the kids were okay and she and Jim hadn't got in yet then. But Danny seemed to have everything under control."

"Yes, he's a good kid. Level-headed."

I nodded. "Responsible, too. He had fed the girls and put them to bed. It must be a relief to Jim to know Danny's so dependable."

"Jim's mother is there now? She must be, I saw Danny get on the school bus."

"Yes. I talked to her a minute this morning."

"That's good." Sylvia took a step closer and lowered her voice slightly. "I heard that Francine ran off with Mason Sturdevant. But I'd think Mason

60

would have more sense than that. Of course, I also heard that she ran off with Orville Patterson."

"With Orville." I was surprised. "Why, she and Orville haven't had a civil word to say to one another since their divorce."

"That's not what I heard."

I remembered that Richanne Worley had told me about the two of them dancing together at a dance in Spray the weekend before. I just stood there, looking receptive, and Sylvia continued.

"I heard that Francine told Virginia Cranston that she wished she'd never left Orville. That would really be something, wouldn't it? If three years and two babies later she decided she'd made a mistake in divorcing Orville and marrying Jim."

"That would be something, all right. I'm not sure what, though." I didn't believe a word of it. For one thing, I couldn't imagine Francine confiding a thing like that to Virginia Cranston. Even in a camp of a hundred people, there are layers of prestige. I couldn't remember a single instance of a close friendship between the wife of a cat-skinner and the wife of a timber-faller. And Francine was more aware of class distinctions than most. She had always considered herself a cut above the rest of us, having been raised in a city somewhere in California, Sacramento or Bakersfield, I think. She

61

didn't have any really close friends in Camp Five or Kinzua. Not women friends, anyway. For another thing, I knew she was having an affair with Mason Sturdevant.

Sylvia went to break up a little friction that had developed on the playground when one of the second-grade boys ground a slab of crusty snow into the face of one of the first-grade girls. She scolded the boy and comforted the girl, who was crying lustily, then she sent the girl into the schoolhouse to wash her face.

"Then, again, I heard that Francine and Mason Sturdevant have been seeing each other on the sly," she said, taking up where she'd left off.

"Not an easy thing to do with him living in Kinzua and her here."

"Well, no, not easy. But certainly not impossible. Especially, since she and Jim go to all the dances in a radius of a hundred miles. I know for a fact that she and Mason met at Pioneer Park a month or so ago. Max saw them."

Max is Sylvia's husband and an acute observer of human nature. I don't know why women have the reputation of being gossips -- the men are every bit as bad.

"Maybe they both just happened to stop there at the same time," I offered. I didn't expect Sylvia to believe it and, for that matter, I didn't believe it myself. "After all, coincidences do happen."

"Sure, they do. And if you think Francine and Mason meeting at Pioneer Park was a coincidence, more power to you."

I smiled at her. "No, I don't really think that. But I don't know what to think about this disappearance of hers."

"It's a puzzler, all right." Sylvia glanced at her watch and blew her whistle. The kids in the lower four grades hurried into the school, leaving their boots and coats in the porch and making a tremendous amount of racket in doing so. As soon as they were inside their schoolroom, I blew my whistle and the older children trooped inside.

They applied themselves pretty well until lunchtime when we all went home to eat. The noon sun glinting off the snow was so bright that I had to squint my eyes even to see. There was a small plate of pecan bars covered with wax paper on my table that I knew Aunt Genevieve must have left on her way to the store or to visit one of her friends. I fixed myself a bologna sandwich and a glass of pineapple juice for lunch. The pecan bars were delicious.

I stopped to get the library books out of my car on the way back to school. I'd forgotten them that morning in my worry about Danny and the girls.

The afternoon went pretty smoothly. I gave Dottie and Debbie the science books and they thanked me in Quoskeen -- I think they thanked me.

Chapter 5

On my way home from school, I met Betty Chichester who was coming down the hill with a small bag of groceries. We exchanged greetings and I commented that I hadn't seen her for some time. Mrs. Chichester is of my parents' generation and I've never known her particularly well. Most of the women who lived at Camp Five wore house dresses and lipstick and combed their hair. Mrs. Chichester wore frocks and the full complement of makeup from eyebrow pencil and mascara to rouge and two shades of foundation. Too, she didn't have a hair-do, she had a coiffure. Her daughter Carleen was a close friend of my cousin Lorraine and I knew her quite well. The only one of the Chichesters' children still at home was their youngest, a daughter named Eileen, who was a senior at Wheeler County High. I didn't know her very well, either, as she was too young to hang out with Lorraine and Carleen and me when we were girls.

I hadn't seen Carleen since a bunch of us had

gone out to sight in the rifles just before hunting season started. Carleen and her husband, Don Burch, had been there and six or eight others. I remembered how Carleen had teased Don about out-shooting him. Guy Blevens and Jim Morton had egged her on until she snatched up Don's thirty-ought-six and put holes in five of the six cans the guys had set on a log as targets. There had been a lot of laughter and bantering back and forth about it but I wasn't sure it was entirely good-natured on Carleen's part. She had always been competitive and winning was paramount to her, regardless of the importance or triviality of the objective. As a matter of fact, I'd always thought she married Don right after high school graduation because he had dated both her and Terry Lindley and she couldn't bear to have people think that Terry could take him away from her. She and Don lived in Kinzua and they seemed as compatible as most married couples. But, then I didn't really see much of them, just glimpses at dances or the store now and then.

"Do you have time to come in for a cup of tea?" Mrs. Chichester asked.

I was rather surprised by the invitation and hesitated, wondering why she had issued it. She had never before invited me to partake of afternoon tea. Under her pleasant manner I thought I could see that she was worried or uneasy so I accepted.

"Of course. I'd love to."

We turned in at her gate and I saw her glance at the house next door. The Chichesters live in the last house in the row so their only next door neighbors are the Mortons. I left my galoshes on the front porch and held the groceries for Mrs. Chichester while she removed hers. Fritz, their old weimeraner, met us at the front door and greeted Mrs. Chichester with restrained ecstasy. She carried her galoshes through the living room and kitchen to put them on her back porch. I set the grocery bag on the kitchen counter and patted the dog on the head. That pleased him and he galloped off to fetch a rubber ball for us to play with.

"Let me have your coat," she said. She laid it over the back of a chair in the living room, motioning me to take another. "I'll just slip out and put the kettle on."

I heard her fill the kettle and rattle the paper bag as she took her groceries out and put them away. Fritz sat in front of me with the ball in his mouth, thumping his tail on the carpet hopefully. I took the ball and rolled it across the room. Fritz gave me a disgusted look, letting me know that he was disappointed in my ball-playing skills. He lay down with the ball between his front paws and rested his chin on it, staring at me balefully. Mrs. Chichester brought in a plate of home-made doughnuts -- the cake kind -- and set them on the occasional table beside me. Presently she returned with two cups of tea and set them down.

"Do you take anything in your tea?" she asked.

I shook my head and she sat down in an armchair on the other side of the little table.

"Help yourself to a doughnut," she said, holding out the plate. "I make them for lunches but I often have a little snack in the afternoon."

"Thank you." I took one and bit into it. It was kind of dry but otherwise it was pretty good. I like them with chocolate frosting on them. I glanced at Fritz but he apparently knew better than to expect to share in high tea. He stretched out on his side and seemed to take no further interest in us.

"I'm sure you're wondering what I'm up to," she said with a little laugh. She didn't sound amused, though.

"Well, as a matter of fact..."

She didn't wait for the rest of my sentence. "It's Francine Morton. I'm worried about her."

"Yes, a lot of people are. As far as I know, Jim hasn't said anything to anyone about where she's gone or why."

She nodded vigorously. "That's exactly it. Why

68

hasn't he? Surely it would be the natural thing to say she's gone to visit her folks or to Portland for some shopping or whatever."

"You would think so. Francine didn't say anything to you about a possible trip? You saw as much of her as anyone, with her living next door."

"Well, there's a road that separates our yards so it's not like we were right cheek by jowl. And she was never much one for dropping over for a few minutes now and then. But it has seemed to me lately that she's been moody and depressed. I saw her walking along the edge of the meadow a time or two this week and she has never done that before."

Mrs. Chichester paused and gave me a look as if she expected me to say something profound. Unfortunately, I couldn't think of anything profound.

"What are you thinking?" I asked. "That she might have fallen and broken a leg?"

She looked a little startled, as if that hadn't occurred to her, but she nodded. "It's possible. She may have had some kind of accident in the woods."

I looked her in the eye and knew that wasn't her real concern. I said as much and she shook her head slowly back and forth. Fritz sat up and looked first at Mrs. Chichester, then at me. He stood up and came over to stand by his mistress, looking up into her face worriedly. She patted him and told him everything was okay. He looked doubtful and lay down with his chin on one of her shoes.

"You're right, Marge. What I'm really afraid of is that she might have committed suicide."

That startled me. Somehow I had never connected a death wish with the vibrant personality of Francine Morton. "Suicide. Francine?"

"I know she's never been happy here in Camp Five. In fact, she's never really liked being away from the city. She was a concert pianist, you know. She had big hopes for a career before she came to Oregon."

"Even so. I mean, I'd think it would take more than a vague unhappiness to make her commit suicide."

"Maybe there was more to it than that." Mrs. Chichester looked morose. "Look, Marge, I don't like to spread unfounded gossip but I've been worried about Francine and Jim lately. Things don't seem to have been going very well with them. I heard them quarrelling one day when Jim was working on that room addition he's building on the house. It seemed a very serious quarrel from the little I heard. I didn't eavesdrop purposely but I was working in the yard and she was practically screaming. I couldn't help but hear."

70

Mrs. Chichester looked miserable enough; I thought she was probably telling me the truth about not wanting to eavesdrop. On the other hand, she'd evidently stayed to listen once the fireworks began to go off.

"I don't know what to say." I searched my mind for something to comfort her with as that was evidently why she'd chosen me to confide in. "I've never been married, as you know, but I believe all married couples quarrel occasionally. It seems to be part and parcel of the married state."

"That's true. We all fuss from time to time. Even Carleen and Don. She's been here twice this week to tell me how impossible he is. But it's just the normal give and take of marriage and that's what I keep telling her." Mrs. Chichester shook her head and smiled tolerantly at her daughter's exaggeration. "You've relieved my mind, Marge. Even if it was a serious quarrel between Jim and Francine, there's no reason to think she would commit suicide over it. It's far more likely that she's simply gone for a shopping trip or even left Jim."

"I think so, Mrs. Chichester. Although I don't see how she could leave for good without her little girls. She's probably just gone to Portland. Or California for a while. I'm sure Jim knows where she is only he's so close-mouthed about his business that he hasn't told anyone."

"As far as leaving the little girls, if she's gone back to California to resume her career, it would make sense for her to leave the children."

"I guess it would, from her perspective. I don't know much about her as a mother. The girls always look clean and well cared for."

"Yes, she's a good mother from that aspect. I don't see her playing with them very often but then they didn't spend a lot of time outside last summer. Francine isn't much of an outdoors girl herself. Well, Marge, you have relieved my mind. I'm glad you could stop in and we could have this little chat."

Recognizing this as the end of our conversation, I stood up and put my coat on and picked up my bundle of papers. "Yes, so am I. I'd better be getting home now. I've got papers to grade."

Mrs. Chichester walked to the door with me. "Come again soon."

I nodded and went out, reflecting that I didn't really like Mrs. Chichester much. A selfish woman with little personal charm.

My stomach was still a little tender from the porcupine quills so I treated myself to an evening of pure sloth. I had a length of silvery pongee with a floral pattern of pink and pale green that I was going to make into a dress for dances and festive occasions and I had thought of cutting it out that night but I just wasn't in the mood. I made a salmon loaf out of a can of sockeye that my brother had caught and had canned on a fishing trip to Reedsport. I didn't have a lemon so while it was baking I walked up to the store.

Lewis and Kathleen Schuyler operate the Camp Five branch of the company store. It's a little building, about the size of my house, with one room of groceries and a lean-to in the back for storage. There's a gas pump out front and a section of mail boxes just inside the door. Lewis was behind the counter, at this time of day Kathleen would be home cooking supper and keeping their two little girls out of mischief. It was almost closing time so I reassured Lewis that I only wanted a lemon, I'd be out in a minute or two.

"I guess I'm not in such a big hurry that you need to hustle yourself, Marge," he laughed. "Take your time."

"Isn't this some weather for this early in the year?"

"Sure is. I expect it'll thaw and we'll have mud now until after Thanksgiving."

I went around behind the mail boxes and pulled my mail out. There wasn't much and I flipped through it to see that there wasn't anything particularly interesting then stuck it in my pocket. The fresh fruits and vegetables were on a wide corner shelf and a glance was enough to show me that of the three lemons, two could be called fresh only because they weren't canned or frozen. I picked up the third one and paid Lewis for it.

"I'll be going after supplies tomorrow," he said. "Is there anything special you'd like for me to get?"

"I can't think of a thing," I said. "Unless it would be apples. Aunt Genevieve likes them and you haven't had any for some time. Only, I don't want to have to buy a whole box if they don't sell." I grinned at him and he laughed.

"I won't hold you responsible. Apples are already on the list, both sweet and cooking apples."

"Have a good trip," I said and went outside.

It felt warmer going down the hill than it had going up. I thought it was probably the effect of Lewis' suggestion of warmer weather coming. I hate to admit it, even to myself, but I am quite suggestible. Camp Five keeps early hours since the men have to be up so early to get out in the woods by first light. The crummies had come back about 4:30 in the afternoon and I knew that most families would be sitting down to supper around 5:00. I saw the men straggling over to the cookhouse as I went down the hill. Everything was just as usual, which gave me a feeling of security. A car turned to come down the hill into camp just as I reached my house. I stood on my steps and watched, curious to see who it was. It was only Carleen Chichester. Or rather, Carleen Burch. She pulled up in front of her folks' house and she and Eileen got out. Probably Eileen had stopped to visit or missed the school bus and Carleen had brought her home.

After supper, when the dishes were done, I sat down at the table to grade the papers that I'd been putting off. Arithmetic and geography and spelling were easy, if sometimes rather comical, because it was a simple matter of fact. Writing exercises were more complicated because they required a certain measure of concentration to grade for spelling, punctuation, grammar, and story in each paper. Usually, I enjoyed reading pupils' little stories and essays. Each child had either something unique to say or a unique way to have his or her say. Tonight my thoughts kept skittering off to the puzzle of the disappearance of Francine Morton. From there they would replay my conversation with Danny on the way home from Kinzua. Then scraps of other conversations would intrude -- gossip and suppositions and insinuations.

I forced myself to stick with my paper grading until I was finished. Then I jumped up. I wanted some kind of action, movement. A walk in the moonlight. The moon was full, intermittently reflecting brightly off the snow, as it played hide and seek with the scudding clouds. It was nearly ten o'clock and most of the houses were completely dark as I walked down to the upper street and along it to the end, then turned and walked back along the lower street. Just past the Mortons' the old road to Kinzua began its narrow, winding way through the forest. For foot traffic, no particular care was needed in daylight; at night, without steady moonlight, I'd have to watch my step. It was a very pretty road, especially here near camp. It was quite a steep grade at the beginning, probably it was about all the old Model A and Model T Fords could pull. The kids used it for sledding and it gave them a glorious run for about a quarter of a mile in a long sweet curve. It brought my own sledding days back with a rush and I wished I had a sled -- I've have swooshed down the hill in an instant.

We used to pour water down it after it was well packed and that gave us such a start that the rest of the ride was just a blur of white. I approached the head of the track carefully, and it was well that I did because these kids had been pouring water down it, too. I kept to one side where the snow was trampled from the kids dragging their sleds back up the hill.

The walking was a little rough but not really hard going. The air was crisp and clean and the stars were awe-inspiring in their remote glitter in the interstices of the clouds. I could feel myself begin to relax under the spell of nature's timeless serenity. The walk back uphill to my house should be just strenuous enough to tire me so I could sleep without a lot of tossing and turning.

I was almost at the bottom of the hill when I heard a human sound. I'm not sure why I immediately identified it as human. It could have been a deer or an elk or even a cougar. It was an indefinite kind of sound. Like an indrawn shuddery breath. It wasn't loud but in the silence when I'd supposed myself to be the only person awake in about a thousand square miles, an owl ruffling her feathers would have drawn my attention. I stopped and stood still, holding my breath. Another sound, off to my right, the sound of something crunching in the snow. I hesitated, drawing a deep breath, then softly asked, "Is anybody there?"

I couldn't see anything in the trees or the shadows of the trees but the crunching of the snow told its own story. Something or someone was just off the road in a little thicket of young fir trees, moving quickly away from the road. I stepped off the road and into the shadow of a big ponderosa pine and listened in growing fright as whatever it was crashed through the buck brush, up the hill. I knew, without consciously reasoning it out, that the some*thing* was some*one*. An animal would have moved away from me and away from camp, this person was moving toward camp, through the trees, skirting the schoolyard.

I lost the sound of whoever it was crashing through the brush and crunching through the snow and was at once profoundly relieved and scared nearly out of my wits. I was afraid to go back to camp in case whoever it was would ambush me. But I was also afraid to stay where I was or go to see what had been happening in that thicket of fir trees. I breathed a little prayer for guidance and protection and finally gathered enough courage to go and look.

Slowly, as quietly as possible, I moved toward the thicket. I listened as hard as I could but there was only the sound of my own breathing and the crunch of the snow under my own galoshes. I stopped every couple of steps to listen but there was nothing. I didn't have far to go. Although I had been half-expecting to find something extraordinary and distasteful among the firs, I was astounded to see a body sprawled across a child's sled. It was dark among the firs so I snapped on my flashlight. It was a woman's body but the face was turned away from me. I stared at it a long time before I could get myself to move in closer. My mind was completely numb. There were no thoughts except for the simple recognition that there was a woman's body on the sled. I don't know how long I stood there before the next thought came, that I must see who it was.

Chapter 6

I walked around the sled, making a wide arc to give myself plenty of leeway between her feet and mine. She was wearing socks but no shoes. I thought it was foolish of her to come out in the snow that way, she would get frostbitten toes. My mind gave itself a shake, to get rid of the ridiculous and prepare for identification. I didn't recognize the dress and that gave me the courage to finally look at the face. It was Mrs. Morton. Jim's mother. My first reaction was a letting down of the guard I had set against the expected onslaught of the horror of recognition. The other thoughts and emotions crowded in quickly. Compassion, sorrow, fear, bewilderment, and the big three: who, how, and why. I didn't see any weapon, no knife or club, nor could I see any blood except for a long ragged scrape on her left arm. Suddenly, fear became my overmastering emotion. I turned and fled up the hill, slipping as I broke through the icy crust of the snow, almost falling half a dozen times before I reached Uncle Miles' house and began to bang on the door.

The door wasn't locked, no one ever bothered to lock a door in Camp Five. I turned the knob and flipped on the overhead light. As I did so, Uncle Miles came into the living room in his long johns and bare-footed.

"Margie." His indignant irritation at being yanked from sleep gave way instantly to concern. "What is it, Margie? What's wrong?"

Oblivious to my galoshes on Aunt Genevieve's oriental rug, I ran to him and flung myself on his chest, sobbing and gasping for breath. Uncle Miles held me to him and patted my back, murmuring that everything was okay. Aunt Genevieve came in, wrapped in a thickly quilted housecoat.

"Margie? What on earth is the matter?" I looked at her and a brisk nurse looked back at me.

Aunt Genevieve knew how to treat trauma victims of all kinds. She gave my shoulder a little shake. I stepped back and Uncle Miles released me. Aunt Genevieve took my hand.

"Mercy, you're cold as ice, Margie. Come in here and sit down." Aunt Genevieve led me into the kitchen.

"No, you don't understand. Mrs. Morton is dead. Down at the foot of the sledding hill."

Uncle Miles frowned. "Jim's wife?" He leaned forward, "At the foot of the hill?"

I shook my head. "Not Francine, his mother."

"His mother?" Whatever Uncle Miles might have expected, that was not it. "What to do you mean, Margie? Maybe she's only fainted or something."

Aunt Genevieve started for her bedroom. "I'll get dressed and go see. Maybe I can do something."

"I'll go with you." Uncle Miles looked at me doubtfully and started after Aunt Genevieve.

"Listen," I begged. "Please, listen. She lying on her back on a Flexible Flyer in the little thicket of fir trees at the bottom of the hill. She's dead."

"Some kind of accident, you mean?" Uncle Miles was scowling at me again.

Aunt Genevieve came back and patted my arm. "You aren't making sense, Margie. Mrs. Morton wouldn't go sledding in the middle of the night."

"Of course she wouldn't," I said impatiently. "I can't imagine what kind of accident could account for it. She isn't wearing a coat or galoshes, just a dress. She isn't even wearing shoes. I heard someone in the thicket and when I went to look, there she was. Dead."

Uncle Miles shook his head. "You stay with Margie, Genevieve. I'll go see what's happened."

Aunt Genevieve nodded and Uncle Miles went into the bedroom. Aunt Genevieve put some stovewood in the trash burner, which still had some coals glowing. They caught and flames broke out along their edges. She put the lid back on and set the tea kettle on it. Then she went out to the back porch and brought Uncle Miles' coat and boots in to warm them.

A few minutes later Uncle Miles came in, fully dressed. He sat down and pulled his boots on.

"I'd better take a blanket," he said, lacing his boots.

Aunt Genevieve brought an old army surplus blanket. Uncle Miles buttoned his coat and, taking the blanket and a flashlight, went to the back door.

"You girls better stay here. I'll be back as soon as I can."

He went out and Aunt Genevieve went to the cupboard and took out a couple of cups and saucers. She set them on the table along with spoons and a quart of milk. I sat down at the kitchen table and began to shake. I pulled my coat tightly around me but I felt chilled and dazed. The teakettle started to whistle and Aunt Genevieve whisked it off the trash burner and filled our cups with boiling water. She dropped a teabag in each one and sat down.

"Now, Margie," she said, "tell me what this is all

about. Why, you're shaking and just as white as snow."

I continued to dip my teabag up and down in the cup from sheer automatism. Aunt Genevieve fixed hers with sugar and milk then took the teabag away from me and put some sugar in my cup.

"Drink that," she ordered.

I don't like sugar in my tea but arguing with Aunt Genevieve when she's in one of her take-charge moods is an exercise in futility. I sipped the tea.

"Now, begin at the beginning and just tell me about it. Start with what you were doing out there in the middle of the night."

"It isn't really the middle of the night," I said, glancing at my watch. I was surprised to see that it wasn't even eleven o'clock yet. It seemed incredible that so much could have happened in something less than forty-five minutes. "I was restless so after I finished grading some papers, I decided to take a walk. I went to the end of the upper street and then to the other end of the lower street. The moonlight was bright so I could see to walk alongside the sledding run and I went down the hill a little ways. When I got to the bottom, I heard something in those firs." I had to stop and take a deep breath before I could steady myself to go on. Aunt

84

Genevieve patted my hand encouragingly.

"Okay, honey," she said. "Then what?"

"Well, I stood and listened. I didn't know if it was a deer or what. Then it started up the hill and made a lot of racket going through the brush."

Aunt Genevieve raised her eyebrows, "Up the hill?"

I nodded. "That's what made me go see what was in the thicket. I knew it wasn't likely that a deer would go towards camp. And I couldn't think of any good reason for a person to be there. I mean, I know I was there, but not in the trees. Anyone might take a walk but no one would want to walk in the dark, among the firs, in about a foot of crusted snow. Would they?"

"I wouldn't think so," she said. "You've had an awful shock, honey. Drink the rest of your tea and I'll get you a nightie. You can sleep in Lorraine's old room."

"Thanks, Aunt Genevieve. But I don't want to be a coward. I'll go on home."

Aunt Genevieve eyed me doubtfully. "Better wait until Miles comes back."

"Yes, I will." Telling Aunt Genevieve about it had taken some of the horror out of it and I had stopped shaking.

Aunt Genevieve stoked the trash burner and put

85

a pot of coffee on to perk. We talked desultorily until, after what seemed like a very long time, Uncle Miles came back. We heard him on the back porch and a minute or two later he came into the kitchen without his coat and boots.

He looked tired and shocked and determined.

"There was nothing anyone could do," he said, answering Aunt Genevieve's inquiring look. "Mrs. Morton was dead. I found her just as you described her, Margie."

"You've told Jim?" Aunt Genevieve asked.

"Yes. I went and got Cory Blevens and Rich Peterson to help me get her up the hill. And on the way back down, I stopped and got Jim. I never hated to tell anyone anything so bad in my life. He thought she was visiting Eloise Troupe or Richanne Worley. She had been good friends with both of them at different times."

"How did he take it?" Aunt Genevieve asked. "Is he all right? Should I go over there? Maybe he needs some help with the babies."

"He's okay. Danny woke up, too, and Jim left him with the babies. He wanted to go to his grandmother but Jim wouldn't let him. They were both pretty torn up."

"What do you think happened?" Aunt Genevieve wondered. "How in the world did she get to the foot

86

of the hill? And on a sled, of all ridiculous things."

Uncle Miles shook his head. "We couldn't see any injury, except that scrape on her arm. I felt her head and I think she may have been hit with something; one place on the back of her head seems to be indented. But I'm not sure."

Aunt Genevieve got him a cup of coffee and Uncle Miles took out his Luckies and the Zippo lighter that Phil had given him for Christmas years ago. He sat down and lit a cigarette; Aunt Genevieve got him an ashtray and sat down across from me. She reached over and put her hand over mine.

"What did you do with," I hesitated, trying to phrase my question softly. But it was not a question that had any softness. "With the body? You brought it up the hill and then where?"

"We took her to the truck shop. There's that little room partitioned off at the back where all the first aid stuff is stored. There's a folding cot and we opened it up and put her on that." He looked uncertainly at Aunt Genevieve. "I left that blanket over her."

"Of course," she said. "You couldn't have done anything else."

"Uncle Miles, how did she die?"

Uncle Miles shook his head. "It looks like she

was hit on the back of the head but I don't really know, Margie. I expect there'll have to be an autopsy. Cory is driving into Kinzua to notify Mr. Hamilton and call the police."

I nodded, it was the only thing to do. I stood up. "I'd better go and let you get back to bed so you can get a little sleep before you have to go to work."

"Tomorrow's Saturday," Uncle Miles reminded me.

"You'd better stay here tonight," Aunt Genevieve said.

"I'm okay," I protested. "Nothing has happened to me. And I could always come back, if I needed to, couldn't I?"

She smiled. "Of course, you could. You know that."

"You'd better stay here tonight, Margie." Uncle Miles said.

I smiled at them both. "I'm okay. Thanks anyway."

Uncle Miles shook his head at me, disapproving of my stubbornness and at the same time approving of my independent spirit. "I'll walk you home, then."

He crushed out his cigarette and Aunt Genevieve warmed his coat while he pulled on his boots again.

"Thanks." I was grateful. I knew that I was going to be scared for a long time and I was glad that

Uncle Miles would be with me when I opened the door and went inside my little house. I was also glad that I had left the living room light burning. I wasn't going to be comfortable in the dark for awhile.

I gave Aunt Genevieve a kiss on the cheek. "I'm sorry about tracking up your floors," I apologized.

She make a dismissive sound and followed us to the door.

"Better lock up," Uncle Miles said to her. "We don't know just what we've got here yet."

"You think she was murdered, don't you?" I blurted out.

"Well, honey, let's just say I don't think Mrs. Morton went down the hill on that Flexible Flyer for the fun of it."

He took my elbow and steered me down the porch steps and out to the road. He very sweetly went inside with me and looked in my closet and behind the bedroom door and under my bed. Laughing rather shakily, I thanked him and he kissed my cheek and left, telling me to lock the door behind him.

I turned up the thermostat on the oil burner then took off my coat and galoshes and wiped up the melted snow from the linoleum. I went into the bedroom and undressed. My abdomen still showed the puncture marks and discoloration but the bruises were turning green and yellow and it was hardly tender at all. I put on some thick flannel pajamas and my warmest chenille robe and curled up on the couch with the afghan over my feet. I knew I wouldn't sleep yet awhile so I opened my Bible and began to read.

It was only a minute or two before I realized that my mind wasn't working in tandem with my eyes. What I was thinking about was Mrs. Morton and that word I'd blurted out -- *murder*. The whole thing was grotesque. Murder in our little community? Impossible. The population in Camp Five stayed right at one hundred people. Except for some of the bachelors, I knew them all and saw most of them every day of my life. There were no murderers amongst them. There couldn't be.

Take Cory Blevens and Rich Peterson, to whom Uncle Miles had gone for assistance in the present emergency. They were both in their thirties, self-reliant, tough, and strong. Strong in both body and character. Cory was a cat-skinner on the construction crew and Rich was the jammer operator on Mr. Chichester's side. They worked hard and collected what they earned but they expected no particular favors from anyone. They were used to solving their own problems. All that was typical of all of us who lived at Camp Five.

Only now it looked like outsiders would have to solve our problem for us. We could grapple with murder but the laws were formulated to take that problem out of our hands and place it in the hands of the police.

That was a new idea for me. The idea of police in Camp Five. I never had seen a policeman in Camp. Once in a while a game warden would come around but I'd never seen nor heard of either the Wheeler County Sheriff's department nor the Oregon State Police in camp. Well, one or the other and maybe both would be in camp tomorrow morning.

There were no police in Kinzua, either. There was a telephone. In fact, there were several. Cory would go to the superintendent's home, of course. Probably he would let Mr. Hamilton phone the police. I didn't know who else had phones. Maybe no one. There wouldn't be anyone at the company office in the middle of the night and he had to notify Mr. Hamilton anyway.

Feeling wide awake, I got up and went over to a window and looked out at the moonlight gleaming on the snow. It was breath-takingly lovely until the thought of footprints intruded. Although there was a crust on the snow, it was not so thick that it would support an adult's weight. It made walking very tiring and irritating, breaking through that crust at every step. It was also noisy and that was one of the reasons it had been so easy for me to hear whoever had been in the fir thicket going back up the hill to camp. Such footprints are not very easy to read, but they should tell us something about the person who made them. And forensic scientists could probably tell quite a lot. If any forensic scientists were sent to examine them. Thinking about that made me realize that there was very little evidence at the scene. The sled and the body itself and those footprints. There hadn't been any blood aside from the scrape on her arm. I didn't think Mrs. Morton had been strangled. There was certainly no cyanosis -- her face wasn't blue and her tongue wasn't black and protruding. She was just lying on the sled, looking peaceful, as if she'd gone to sleep there. I shuddered, wishing I'd asked Aunt Genevieve for some sleeping tablets.

The moon suddenly got much dimmer. That seemed very strange to me for a moment. I wondered if the man in the moon had forgotten to pay his electric bill. I glanced up at the sky. The phenomenon was entirely natural. The clouds had thickened, once more covering the whole sky.

My mind reverted to Mrs. Morton. It showed me just how they would have placed the cot in the little first aid room and how they would place Mrs.

Morton on the cot. I knew Uncle Miles had covered her with a blanket. That seemed almost funny. There was no heat in the little room. No amount of blankets could prevent Mrs. Morton from freezing stiff. But that didn't matter because rigor mortis would set in any time now and she would be completely stiff from that. I wondered if freezing temperatures would affect the rigor. I wanted my mind to shut down. I didn't want to think these ridiculous thoughts. Thank goodness I hadn't stayed with Aunt Genevieve. What if I had said these things to her? She would think I'd flipped my lid.

I knew why Aunt Genevieve hadn't insisted on going with Uncle Miles. As a nurse, she might have thought there would be something she could do. But Uncle Miles had been through World War II and they had both seen death many times. She knew that Uncle Miles would bring Mrs. Morton to her if there was anything she could do.

Headlights appeared and dropped down the road into camp. Cory Blevens was back from Kinzua. I looked at the clock. Twenty minutes after two. Cory wouldn't get much sleep. I left one of the living room lamps on, checked to make sure my door was locked, and went to bed.

Chapter 7

Saturday morning I woke to see that the snow was still falling. After being awake most of the night, I had slept heavily through the small hours of the morning. I was frightened. I didn't really believe there was a homicidal maniac loose in Camp Five who might sneak up on me any moment and add me to his list of victims. But someone had undoubtedly killed Mrs. Morton and I couldn't imagine a reason for it. Not a real reason. That such an ordinary, nice, pleasant elderly woman had an enemy who had trailed her to Camp Five and done her to death was an idea so outrageously illogical that I could almost laugh about it. The only reason I could imagine for anyone to kill Mrs. Morton was if she had known what had happened to Francine. And since I didn't know what had happened to Francine, that was simply a dead end.

Nevertheless, every time I closed my eyes, I saw a mental picture of Mrs. Morton lying on the sled in the fir thicket. That would lead to a mental review of the whole sequence of events -- running to Uncle Miles and telling him and Aunt Genevieve about it. Then I'd go over the possibilities of who and why until I was exhausted and began to doze off. At which point, I would jerk awake and begin all over again.

When I wakened at six, I decided to get up and begin the day. At least I would have things to distract me whenever my mind tried to show me that fir thicket again. I hurriedly thrust my feet into slippers and pulled my galoshes on. Not bothering with a bathrobe, I put my coat on and dashed over to the women's bath house. My usual occupation on Saturday mornings is to take my laundry over to Aunt Genevieve's and do my washing. However, with the snow coming down as it was, there was no point in it that Saturday. So I had an unexpectedly idle Saturday morning.

I dressed and fixed myself a bowl of oatmeal and a glass of pineapple juice. I didn't bother about firing up the trash burner, but put a teakettle full of water on the electric range to heat to do the dishes with. As I ate, I reflected that the Morton household was bereaved and I would have to take them some kind of food. I wondered if Francine had heard the news of her mother-in-law's death and if so, if she would be coming home. Or maybe Francine had been the first victim. That thought brought back the confusion and horror of the night before and I shied away. I decided to make a tamale pie and take it to the Mortons. I knew Jim was fond of the dish but even if he threw it out untasted, it was necessary that I take them something.

Checking the contents of my cupboards, I found that I had all the necessary ingredients except hamburger. I put on my outdoor things and tied a scarf around my head. I hated wearing a scarf but I felt the need for some kind of head covering. As I walked up the hill to the store, the Miller twins caught up with me.

"Hi, Miss O'Connor," they greeting me in unison.

"Hi. What are you girls up to this morning?"

"We're detecting. Mrs. Morton was murdered last night and we're going to find out who did it," answered Debbie.

"You found her, didn't you? That's what Mom said," added Dottie.

"Yes, I found her. It was horrible."

"Why?" Both girls looked at me in a puzzled fashion. Death was new to them and they hadn't realized that death by murder had many ramifications beyond the simple fact of death.

"Why?" I smiled at them. "Well, it was a shock,

96

you know. And then I heard someone going away, up the hill, in the dark."

"The murderer, you mean?" breathed Dottie.

"I suppose so. I don't know who else it would have been."

The girls exchanged significant looks and broke into a spate of Quoskeen. I left them to it and went into the store. Lewis was behind the counter, talking to Eloise Troupe and Mark Cranston.

"Oh, here she is now," Lewis said. "Hi, Marge. We were just talking about Mrs. Morton and how you found her."

"Hi," I said, nodding to include them all.

Mrs. Troupe stared at me avidly. "Did you really find her?"

"Yes, I'm afraid so."

Mr. Cranston set a can of coffee down on the counter. "In the middle of the night? What were you doing out there in the middle of the night? That's what I don't get."

"Well, I was just feeling kind of restless and I went for a little walk." I could hear myself sounding defensive and I tried to stop it. "It wasn't snowing hard and now and then the moon broke through the clouds. It was beautiful with the moonlight on the snow. It wasn't really the middle of the night. It was only about ten o'clock."

Mr. Cranston shook his head and I could see that I wasn't making any sense as far as he was concerned. Debbie and Dottie came in and, seeing the grown-ups in serious conversation, kept very quiet, taking it all in.

"Weren't you scared?" Mrs. Troupe peered into my face so hard that I took a step backwards.

"As a matter of fact, I was. It was quite a relief to get to Uncle Miles' and Aunt Genevieve's."

"It must have been."

Lewis seemed to understand my distress in being interrogated by Mrs. Troupe because he became the brisk storekeeper, asking Mr. Cranston if he needed anything else. Mr. Cranston didn't. He signed for his coffee and left.

"We're going to investigate Mrs. Morton's murder," Dottie announced.

"We've already been down to look at the footprints. We'll have to measure your feet, Miss O'Connor, so we can tell which footprints are yours and which are the murderer's," Debbie said.

"And we have to look at all the men's boots to see which ones are okay and which ones belong to the murderer," Dottie added.

Mrs. Troupe turned her gimlet stare on the girls. "You'll do no such thing." She was indignant. "The very idea. You go on home and behave yourselves.

This is not a game and it is not for little girls to meddle in."

Lewis came to the rescue again, perhaps fearing that the girls would talk back to Mrs. Troupe. "What can I do for you, Mrs. Troupe? I have a new box of oranges. And I picked up some bananas yesterday."

Mrs. Troupe cast a final glare at the twins, then turned to Lewis and smiled graciously. "I just came for a box of raisins," she said. "I'm making cookies and I got the batter mixed up before I saw I was out of raisins. They're for Jim Morton. He's always liked my raisin cookies."

Dottie crossed to the shelf where the raisins were kept, brought a box back and handed it to Mrs. Troupe.

Mrs. Troupe scowled but she took it and Dottie grinned at her sister behind the woman's back as she turned to sign for the raisins.

"Anything else?" Lewis asked.

"No, that's all, thanks." Mrs. Troupe turned to me. "I'll be over sometime today, Marge. I want to talk to you about Ray."

"All right. I should be home pretty much all day."

Mrs. Troupe nodded and went out. The girls immediately broke into Quoskeen, interspersed with much giggling. I frowned at them but I couldn't help but agree with them. Mrs. Troupe was rather trying.

"I need a pound of hamburger, Lewis," I said.

He went to the diminutive meat case and weighed out a pound of the meat. As he wrapped it, Dottie and Debbie calmed themselves and became serious again.

"Do you know when they're going to take Mrs. Morgan away, Mr. Schuyler?" Debbie asked.

"No, I haven't heard what the plans are. I expect the police will make arrangements."

"There'll have to be an autopsy," Dottie remarked.

"Yes, to tell how she was killed and what she ate for supper and what time she was killed and everything," Debbie explained.

"Where do they learn all that stuff?" Lewis asked.

"Don't look at me," I said. "I don't teach crime detection. The books they read don't all come from the school library."

"Thank you for the weather books, Miss O'Connor," said Dottie. "They're lots more interesting than we thought they would be."

"You're welcome," I said. I paid Lewis for the hamburger. As I was not an employee of the company, I was one of the few who paid cash instead of running a bill and having it deducted

100

from my paycheck.

"This snow we're getting comes from nimbostratus clouds," Debbie said informatively.

"Most thunderstorms come from cumulonimbus clouds," Dottie added. "I wish we could have a thunderstorm with snow. I bet lightning in a snowstorm would be supercollosal."

"I've never seen lightning with a snowstorm," I said. "Does it ever happen?"

"Well, according to one of those books," Dottie said, "it does happen sometimes. But it doesn't say how often."

"Or where," Debbie put in. "Some kinds of weather only happen in certain parts of the world. Like monsoons and northern lights."

"The aurora borealis isn't weather," Dottie stated.

I smiled at Lewis and went out, leaving the twins to their argument. I could see I was going to have to get possession of the weather books before I graded their reports or I was apt to make a fool of myself. I hadn't the least idea whether the aurora borealis was weather-related or not. About once in a blue moon, the northern lights were visible from camp. I'd seen them one night when I was about the twins' age. There was a faint sheen of varicolored light that Uncle Miles said was the northern lights. It had been in the winter but I didn't know if they showed only under certain weather conditions.

It didn't take long to make the tamale pie and put it in the oven. As soon as I washed up the cooking utensils, I decided to cut out my new dress. Guy Blevens, Cory's older brother, was going to take me to a dance in Fossil that evening. Guy worked in a haberdashery in Condon. There was no sense in him coming clear out to Camp Five to pick me up and doubling back to Fossil so I was going to ride in with Cory. That is, if the snow didn't make the roads impassable. The snow was too deep for the grasshopper but Ralph Buies would keep the road open between Camp Five and Kinzua, using the rotary snowplow. If it got really deep on Kinzua Mountain and Fossil Hill, though, it might be impractical to travel that road. Especially at night and just for a dance.

I got out my box of patterns and flipped through them. I knew which one I wanted and I had used it before so I wouldn't have the tedium of trimming it and fitting it. It was on the bottom, of course, everything always is. The dress had a sleeveless, fitted bodice with a jewel neckline and a sheath skirt. I thought it would show off the shimmer of the silvery pongee just right.

Usually I played the phonograph while I sewed or cooked and I would have liked some music that morning, too, but it just didn't seem right, after the events of the night before. I stripped the cloth off the table and laid the pongee out, carefully smoothing it and lining up the selvages, as I pinned the flimsy tissue pattern to the cloth. I used the pinking shears to cut it out, marking the darts and zipper insertion points.

There was a knock on the door and I jumped convulsively, my heart pounding. The upper part of the door was glass and I could see Mrs. Troupe. I went and opened the door.

"Come in," I said.

She stepped through the door and I closed it as she stooped to remove her galoshes.

"May I take your coat?"

"You certainly are jumpy." Mrs. Troupe said it as if she disapproved of jumpiness.

She peeled off her coat and handed it to me. I draped it over the back of a kitchen chair and indicated the couch. She sat in the easy chair and I sat on the couch.

"I don't really want to talk about Ray, Marge. It's this murder, I want to talk about."

That surprised me. I didn't see that it was anything special to do with her. As far as I knew, she hadn't been any friend of the Mortons'. I knew she disliked Francine intensely. Then, again, she did everything intensely.

"Why?" I asked bluntly, too surprised to be tactful.

"Lilian Morton was my friend. We both lived in Pondosa years ago, when my boys were small, and we got to be as close as sisters. Jim was married to his first wife then and Danny was just a little kid. I haven't seen much of Lilian since we moved here and she moved over to Plush after her husband died. But we wrote back and forth regular and we stopped in to see her that time we took the boys to the coast."

"I see. I'm sorry, Mrs. Troupe."

"What I want to know is, who killed her? Why? She was a wonderful woman. No one could have hated her."

"I only met her once, briefly yesterday morning. I don't know who killed her."

"You found her." Mrs. Troupe made it sound like an accusation of some kind.

"Yes, I found her. But there was nothing that I could see to point to whoever did it."

I suddenly remembered the tamale pie in the oven. I jumped up and murmured an excuse and whipped the oven door open. The pie was a little overdone but not unduly so. I took it out and set it on a hot pad on the countertop.

104

"Sorry," I said, sitting down again. "I was baking a tamale pie for Jim."

"You were at the Mortons' the night Francine left. In the middle of the night again. You and Jim were seen, you know."

I didn't know but I believed her. Even in the middle of the night someone was bound to see anything there was to see -- someone disturbed by a bad dream or needing bicarbonate of soda or something, and glancing out the window. And it hadn't been the middle of the night when I fell over the porcupine, either. Naturally, whoever had seen Jim walking me home hadn't seen the porcupine.

"I fell over a porcupine and Jim walked me home."

Mrs. Troupe gazed at me intently and suspiciously. "What were you doing out that night? Taking another walk?"

I nodded. "Something like that."

"It seems to be a habit with you, Marge, walking in the middle of the night."

"It wasn't the middle of the night. It was early evening."

"It was snowing, wasn't it? Halloween night?"

"Yes, it was." I was tired of these questions, seeming to put me in a worse and worse light. I had no intention of telling her that I'd had to make a trip to the bath house and heard a cougar scream. Let her think what she liked.

She reverted to the events of the night before. "Was it snowing when you went for your walk last night?"

"No, it had just about stopped. It started again later."

"Didn't you get any look at all of the person you heard going up the hill? You did hear someone going up toward camp, didn't you? That's what someone said."

"Yes, I did hear someone. That's why I went into the thicket of firs. I wondered why anyone would be there at that time of night."

"Couldn't you tell anything about the person, whether it was a man or a woman, at least?"

"No, I didn't see whoever it was at all, I just heard someone moving. I thought at first it must be a deer but when the sound went uphill, I thought it must be a person. Because an animal wouldn't go toward camp, it would go away from human habitation."

Mrs. Troupe frowned. Then she nodded. "Okay, I see. But there's a stretch of open ground between the bottom of the hill and the first houses. Surely, you must have caught a glimpse at least of the person. It was bright moonlight, wasn't it?"

"It was just then. But I really didn't see anyone. At first those firs were between us and then, after I saw Mrs. Morton, I was really too frightened to think clearly for a few minutes."

The sight of Mrs. Morton lying on the sled came back to me and I started to shake. Mrs. Troupe looked at me in a puzzled kind of way.

"What's wrong with you, Marge? Are you all right?"

"No, I'm not all right." Suddenly I was extremely angry. "I don't want to talk about this anymore. I don't ever want to talk about it again. It's horrible."

She looked at me with distaste. "You'd better calm yourself, you know. Hysterics won't do you any good."

She stood up and got ready to go outside while I sat and tried to keep from laughing. I knew that the urge to laugh was borderline hysteria but Mrs. Troupe was so funny with her disapproval and her attempt at the third degree that it was hard to keep it in. I managed to open the door and tell her goodbye. She gave me a cold stare and went out. I shut the door and collapsed on the couch in a fit of weeping. I kept seeing flashes in my mind's eye of Mrs. Morton and Mrs. Troupe and the moonlight on the snow -- I was frightened and lonely and confused. Nothing made sense.

Chapter 8

It was snowing hard again when I got bundled up to take the tamale pie to Jim. It was nearly lunch time when I knocked on his back door. I could hear the babies crying and Danny and Jim shouting at each other even before Danny opened the kitchen door and erupted onto the back porch. It appeared that he hadn't heard my knock -- I backed off the step and out of the way as he flung the outer door open. He jerked his coat off a hook and turned without even seeing me and shouted at Jim who was coming through the door onto the porch.

"I loved Gramma," Danny shouted. "I loved her and now she's dead and somebody killed her."

"Danny, don't be stupid. Do you want to get me arrested? Come back in here, right now."

Just then Jim saw me standing behind Danny and tried to shush the boy. Danny wasn't about to be shushed.

"Don't worry, I won't tell anyone." Danny whirled, narrowly missed running smack into me, and ran across the road and down the hill into the meadow, pulling his coat on as he went. I'm not sure he ever did see me through the tears that poured down his face. He broke through the crust of the snow with every step after he left the road and he slipped a couple of times as I watched but didn't go clear down.

"Margie." Jim looked at me tiredly. "Come in."

He held the door for me and I went in and handed him the tamale pie. I left my outdoor things on the back porch and closed the inner door behind me as I went into the kitchen. Jim set the pie on the stovetop. There were several covered dishes on the counter and a fruit pie of some kind, probably apple, and a frosted cake. He went on into the living room and picked up Holly, who was standing in the middle of the floor howling. The baby was in her bassinet, also shrieking. I picked her up and cuddled her against me, whispering that it was all right as I patted her. Jim sat on the couch and held Holly, trying to calm her. I saw a box of tissues on an end table and passed them to him.

There was a knock at the back door and I started to answer it. I only got as far as the kitchen door when the outside door opened and through the glass I could see Carleen Burch. She came into the kitchen, carrying a large yellow Pyrex bowl. She stopped when she saw me and I couldn't quite decipher the look on her face. I'd have said she looked angry if there had been anything for her to be angry about.

"Hi, Carleen." I said, over the baby's wailing.

"Marge. Hi." She gestured at the yellow bowl and set it on the counter. "I've brought Jim some venison stew."

I nodded. "He's in here, with Holly."

Carleen went into the living room and touched Jim on the shoulder. He looked up at her and she patted his cheek.

"I'm so sorry, Jim," she said, trying to get a tone of sympathy into her voice as she raised it to carry over the babies' crying.

"Thanks, Carleen." He continued to cuddle Holly and turned his attention back to her.

"You need to eat, Jim. I've brought some stew. I'll heat it up for your lunch," Carleen said.

"I'm not hungry," Jim told her but she either didn't hear him or didn't pay any attention because she went into the kitchen and we could hear her banging pots and pans around.

I sat in Francine's rocking chair and rocked little Misty. We finally got the girls quieted. Misty fell asleep and I looked down at her sweet little face and hoped that life would be good to her and her sister.

Holly looked up at her father and asked, "Mommy?"

"Mommy's not here, honey," he told her gently.

"Where?"

Jim looked at me. "I don't know what to tell her," he whispered. "I just don't know."

Holly squirmed down from Jim's lap and came over to me. She looked up at me with a sort of quizzical trust and asked, "Where Mommy?"

I thought a lie would be better than nothing so I said, as firmly as I could manage, "Your mommy went to visit her mommy, Holly. She missed her mommy and wanted to see her. She'll come home soon."

"Soon?"

"Sure."

Holly stared up at me for a minute and apparently decided that she could trust me. She went back to Jim and patted his knee.

"Mommy soon," she told him, nodding her head.

She trotted off, then, into her bedroom and came back with a little wagon full of small toys that she dumped out on the floor and squatted down to separate into two piles. She seemed to know exactly what she was doing but to me it looked as if she was crooning gibberish and aimlessly moving things from one pile to the other and back again.

111

Misty was sleeping soundly so I stood up and put her in her bassinet, covering her lightly with a little blanket.

"I've got to go, Jim."

"Thanks for coming, Marge. Thanks for bringing the…"

I realized that he had no idea what was under the tea towel in the pan I'd handed him. "Tamale pie," I told him. "I seem to remember that you like tamale pie."

He smiled bleakly. "Yes, I do. Thanks a lot."

He went with me to the back porch and held my coat for me. Carleen was stirring her stew in a pan on the stove and didn't look up as we went through the kitchen, though I could feel her hostility and it puzzled me. Jim patted my shoulder as I slipped my arms into the frigid sleeves of the coat. I turned and looked into his eyes.

"You know I'm sorry about your mother. I only met her once briefly yesterday morning but I could see that she was a wonderful woman."

Jim nodded. "Thanks."

I could see that he didn't want to break down in front of me so I lightly touched his cheek and turned to go.

"Let me know if I can help in any way, Jim. Stay with the babies or anything."

"I will. Thanks."

As he closed the door behind me, I heard Carleen tell him that he needed to keep up his strength and lunch would be ready in a minute.

I went on up the hill to my own house. The snow was almost knee-deep by that time. A freak storm for so early in the winter. When I opened my door, I glanced around nervously, even back over my shoulder although I knew there was no one near me. I looked quickly around the front room and in the bedroom. I even looked in the closet and under the bed. I knew there was no one hiding in my house but just knowing wasn't enough, I had to see it, too. I shivered and took off my coat. The snow was over the tops of my galoshes and my feet were cold and wet; I changed into warm fuzzy slippers.

I fixed myself a peanut butter and jelly sandwich and took it and a glass of pineapple juice into the living room. I usually read while I ate. It didn't seem right to be reading about murder for amusement, not to mention that the very word gave me the horrors, so I picked up a *National Geographic* magazine I hadn't finished. Somehow the Bantu peoples of Africa didn't really grip my attention and neither did recent archeological discoveries in Mesopotamia. Both were subjects that I ordinarily found deeply interesting but with murder in Camp Five, right

113

smack in the middle of my field of vision, there wasn't much else that I could take an interest in.

As soon as I finished eating, I put the magazine down and put my plate and glass in the sink. I would do them up with my dinner dishes. I set up the ironing board and plugged the iron in, setting it on its next to lowest heat. I took the lamp off the top of the sewing machine and moved the photo frames and knick-knacks. It only took a moment to raise the machine and set the foot pedal on the floor. I moved one of the kitchen chairs over and was ready to sew. It didn't take long to put the dress together, all but the zipper and hem. I like to sew but zippers have never been my strong suit. It was a pretty dress, just as pretty as I'd thought it would be. I went to get a drink of water before I tackled the zipper and looked out the window above the sink.

Richanne Worley was plowing her way through the snow, coming to see me. She looked rather grim as she came up the path. I went to the door and opened it just as she raised her hand to knock.

"Come in, Richanne," I said.

"Thank you," she said.

I took her coat and she stooped to unfasten her galoshes.

"The snow is up over the tops of my overshoes, it's worked its way clear down into my shoes."

"I know, I just came in and had the same thing happen. Cold."

I waved her to the easy chair and she sat.

"Well, you know what they say: cold feet, warm heart."

"Cold hands, warm heart."

She shrugged. "Same difference. You know what I mean."

"Would you like a cup of tea?" I asked.

"No thanks. I can only stay a minute."

I sat on the couch and gave her my full attention.

"I don't know how well you knew Lilian Morton but she and I were real good friends. She was about the best woman I ever knew."

Richanne's voice broke and she closed her eyes. It kind of shocked me to see Richanne so nearly in tears. She always seemed so tough, I had never associated her with the softness of weeping. I couldn't think of anything to say. In a minute or so, she resumed.

"Years ago, when my kids and Jim were in grade school, we lived in Sweet Home and so did the Mortons. Lilian was the kind of woman who was always helping someone. If a neighbor was down on their luck, Lilian would see to it that they had food on the table. If someone was sick or hurt, she'd look in on them to make sure they had everything they

115

needed. I've never known her to turn her back on anyone who needed her help in any way, shape, or form. You know the kind of woman I mean?"

"Yes, I know." My own mother had been much like that. She had taken the injunction to be her brother's keeper very literally and in the best way possible.

"So who would want to kill her? No one, that's who. Lilian had no enemies. No one would want to hurt her."

"Still, someone did hurt her," I pointed out, as gently as I could.

"I know. But, listen, maybe it wasn't Lilian they meant to kill. Maybe they mistook her for someone else."

That made sense to me in a way because I hadn't been able to think of anyone who would want to kill Mrs. Morton, either. Only I couldn't see how she could be mistaken for someone else and told Richanne so.

"We don't know where she was actually killed, do we? I mean, I don't suppose she was actually killed in that fir thicket down at the bottom of the sledding hill."

"No, I don't think so, either. I guess I assumed that she was taken there on the sled."

"Whose sled is it?"

"I don't know. It was a Flexible Flyer, that's all I saw."

"Every kid in camp has one. Where is it now?"

"I don't know. Uncle Miles and Cory Blevens and Rich Peterson took her up to the first aid room at the truck shop. I don't know how they got her there or what they did with the sled."

Richanne nodded thoughtfully. "I'll have to find that out." She paused, then said, "When are the police coming?"

"Good heavens, I don't know. How could I know?"

"I thought Miles might have told you."

"I haven't seen Uncle Miles today. Anyway, how would he know when the police are going to get here?"

"He's hand in glove with Hamilton, isn't he?"

"Well -- I guess that's one way to put it."

"Sure he is. Hamilton's the general supervisor and Miles is construction boss. Don't tell me he didn't send Cory Blevens to tell Hamilton and the cops, too."

"Yes, I suppose he did."

"It's funny Hamilton hasn't been out today. I don't mean 'funny, ha-ha,' I mean 'funny, odd, strange.'"

I assured her that I knew what she meant. "But

we don't know that Mr. Hamilton hasn't been here today. At least, I don't."

"Don't be silly, you're the first person he would want to talk to, since you found her."

That made sense. "Are the roads blocked? The snow is pretty deep."

Richanne snorted. "No, the roads aren't blocked. It's a light, dry snow and Ralph is keeping the road to Kinzua clear."

I hadn't really expected that it was the snow that was keeping Mr. Hamilton out of camp. "What do you think, then, Richanne?"

"I don't know what to think. Maybe he's waiting for the cops. If he is, he may wait a long time. They won't want to come clear out here in this storm. Marge, do you have any idea where she was killed? Or who killed her?"

I shook my head. "I'm sorry. I just don't."

"When you went down the hill, did you see any suspicious tracks?"

"No, of course not. If I had, I wouldn't have gone down the hill."

"I heard that you saw someone running out of that little stand of firs where you found her. Did you recognize whoever that was?"

"I didn't see anyone, Richanne. I heard someone. The snow had crusted over, you know, and I heard someone breaking through the crust and crashing through the buck brush. I thought it was a deer at first, but when it went toward camp instead of away, I knew it must be a person. That's why I went into the thicket -- to see what on earth someone was doing in there in the dark."

"It was bright moonlight last night," she reminded me.

"Not all the time and not in the thicket at all. Those trees are so close together that bright sunshine hardly penetrates."

"I can't help but wonder if it has anything to do with Francine."

"Francine?" I didn't want to think about that. "How on earth could it be connected to Francine? You mean her leaving?"

Richanne nodded. "Maybe Francine didn't leave. Maybe she was the first and Lilian ran across something she wasn't meant to see. Or hear."

"Richanne." Although the thought had crossed my mind, I was aghast. "What are you saying? That Jim killed his wife and then his mother? You're making him out a monster."

"Worse things than that happen, Marge. You're young yet and idealistic. You don't know what a terrible place this world can be."

I was indignant. I might be young and maybe I

was naive, but nothing was going to persuade me that Jim was a cold-blooded killer. I thought of him cuddling his baby girl, comforting her. Then the picture of his mother lying dead on the sled in the snow flashed into my mind. I felt I couldn't bear any more of Richanne's speculations.

"It is a terrible place, I agree with you. Especially when we go around suspecting our neighbors of heinous crimes."

"You were seen the other night, you know. You and Jim Morton, walking in the moonlight. You probably thought you were safe enough but someone always sees. You can't hide anything in a place the size of Camp Five."

"Richanne, Jim and I are not having an affair. I happened to meet him right after I fell over a porcupine. He walked me home. That's all. He didn't even come in."

She nodded. "I know. And I believe you but there are some who won't."

"I'm not going to dignify gossip by taking any notice of it."

"I don't know as that's a very sensible attitude, Marge. But you're stubborn, I know that. I just thought you ought to know what's being said. Well, that's what I came to say."

She stood up and pulled on her galoshes. I held

her coat for her.

"I hate the feel of wet galoshes on my feet." She put her coat on. "I've got to get up to the cook shack. I'm fixing a leg of pork for the men's supper."

"'Bye, Richanne. Come again soon."

She turned to look at me seriously. "I will. Be careful, Marge. Even if you didn't recognize anyone, they may think you did."

That gave me food for thought. I closed the door and went to stand over the oil stove, feeling chilled. Then I realized that it wasn't the kind of chill that external heat can affect but a kind of emotional chill. But at least I didn't feel weepy. I hate to cry.

I didn't much care about the new dress after Richanne's visit but I needed something to do. Besides, I have a tendency to begin sewing projects and abandon them before they're finished so I had made it a rule to complete everything I started before going on to the next thing, if it was at all possible. I sat down at the machine and wrestled that dad-blamed zipper until I got it firmly stitched in place. I was feeling almost smug as I ran it up and down to prove that it worked perfectly. I was pressing the hem in when another knock at the door made me jump.

Chapter 9

My heart jumped and began to hammer as I turned to meet whatever threatened at my door. It was Uncle Miles and Pierce Hamilton. I took a deep breath and glanced at my watch as I went to open the door. I was surprised to find that it was only a little before four. This was turning into the longest day of my life. I did not want to go all over last night again but I knew I would have to.

"Mr. Hamilton, Uncle Miles. Come in."

They knocked the snow off their boots and stepped inside. I took their coats and put them over a chair as they said their hellos.

"Margie, I'm sorry to have to bring this up again," Mr. Hamilton began. "I know you must be trying to forget it."

I smiled as brightly as I could at him, but I'm afraid it was a wan attempt.

"It's all right, Mr. Hamilton. I know you have to find out all you can. It's a company town. Please, have a seat."

Mr. Hamilton took the easy chair and Uncle Miles and I sat on the couch.

"The police aren't going to get here today," Mr. Hamilton said. "The phone line is down and I don't know when the repair crew will be able to find the break and repair it. It's probably broken in several places. Two years ago when we had that heavy snow in January, the lines were broken half-a-dozen places. Anyway, it's apt to be a couple of days before anyone can get into either Kinzua or camp from any direction. The road over Fossil Hill is drifted over and every other road in the county is also a mess."

"Well," Uncle Miles chipped in, "people may not be able to get in here but I'll bet we go to work Monday, just as usual."

Mr. Hamilton looked a little surprised. "Of course. I don't know why not. The road between here and Kinzua is okay and Ralph will keep it open. I've got a couple of other men with snowplows working on the roads out in the woods. I don't think there'll be any real problem. It may take a little longer to get out there but that's all."

"Can you radio the police, Mr. Hamilton?" I asked that rather diffidently because I know virtually nothing about two-way radios and how they work.

"No, they're not on the same frequency as we are. Our radios still work and we can communicate with each other but not the outside world."

I nodded to show that I understood. Uncle Miles pulled out his Luckies and Zippo and lit a cigarette. There was an ashtray on the end table beside him.

"Would you like a cup of coffee, Mr. Hamilton? Uncle Miles?"

Mr. Hamilton shook his head. Uncle Miles declined, too.

"Marge, I need to know everything you heard, saw, and did last night when you found Mrs. Morton's body."

I folded my arms across my chest and fought to keep my composure. There was absolutely no reason to get in a tizzy or feel frightened. Nothing was going to happen in my own home with Uncle Miles and Mr. Hamilton right there. I told Mr. Hamilton how I happened to be walking down the sledding hill and why I had gone into the fir thicket and what I'd heard and seen there. I told him how I had fled to Uncle Miles and Aunt Genevieve and turned the responsibility over to Uncle Miles. Mr. Hamilton asked a few questions but he appeared to grasp the essentials.

"I've seen the body," he said, "and been down to the thicket. All the footprints have been snowed

124

over and completely obliterated. Not that we could have told much, if anything, from footprints in that kind of snow anyway. Fluffy with a layer of crust and then more fluff on top. Footprints are just holes in the snow in those conditions."

He stood up. Uncle Miles rose also, and stubbed out his cigarette. I got to my feet and edged over to the chair where the coats were.

"Thanks, Marge," Mr. Hamilton said. "You might want to write it all down while it's still fresh in your memory. I know it won't be a pleasant task, but the police will eventually come around and they'll want a statement."

"I should have thought of that," I said. "I'll do it this afternoon."

They put their coats on and Uncle Miles gave me a kiss on the cheek.

"Keep your chin up, honey," he said. "Come on over to the house if you don't want to be alone."

"I'm okay, Uncle Miles. Thanks."

"'Bye, Marge," said Mr. Hamilton. "I don't think there's anything to worry about but you ought to be careful about walking in the dark and leaving your door unlocked until we find out who did this and why. We don't want you to be the next victim."

"Pierce is right," Uncle Miles said. "Until we find out who did it and why, we all need to take precautions."

"I'll be careful," I promised.

"No more midnight rambles?" Uncle Miles insisted.

I smiled at him. "I'll be most terrifically, terribly careful."

"I'm going over to Miles' and Genevieve's now. I'll be there for an hour or so, I expect, talking it over. If you remember anything else or hear anything that might be helpful, come and tell me. Okay?"

"Okay."

The two men went out and I closed the door behind them. I finished pressing the hem in my dress and sat down to stitch it. Hemming a garment occupies very little of one's attention so I was free to think over the various conversations I'd had that day. That, of course, led me back to the night before and Mrs. Morton lying on the sled.

I wondered if they had found out whose sled it was. And if so, if it helped any. Probably not. All the kids had sleds and most of them were Flexible Flyers. There would be sleds in the garages and woodsheds of people whose children had grown up and moved away, too. I was pretty sure Phil and Lorraine's sleds were still in Uncle Miles' garage -- I'd noticed them hanging on the far wall a year ago

126

when I was helping Aunt Genevieve refinish her coffee and end tables. Uncle Miles had locked that particular sled up in the first aid room with Mrs. Morton to keep any fingerprints for the police.

It was snowing harder than ever. The crying babies had put Danny right out of my mind but now I wondered about him. He had been upset, to say the least, when he had nearly run me down coming out of the house as I was going up the walk. I tried to remember exactly what he had yelled at his father as he ran out. Something about knowing someone had killed her. And Jim. What exactly had Jim shouted after him? I couldn't remember except that he was trying to quiet the boy. But I had the feeling that Danny was accusing Jim of something. Not, surely, of murdering his own mother.

Shocking as that thought was, I had to admit to myself that it was what Danny had seemed to be saying. But why? Why would Danny think Jim had killed Mrs. Morton? There had to be a reason. Something he had seen or heard.

Then there was still the problem of Francine Morton. Of where she had gone and why. She might have run off with another man. That seemed the most likely explanation for her disappearance. Or perhaps she was the first victim and the elder Mrs. Morton was the second. In that case, who had killed

Francine and why? There was no lack of suspects in her case. Unlike her mother-in-law, she had not been the kind of woman whom people looked up to and cherished as friends. There were several men in her life who could conceivably have wanted her dead. She was that kind of woman.

Maybe Mrs. Morton had run across some kind of evidence showing who had killed Francine. That would mean the murderer was a member of the family. Because Mrs. Morton hadn't been there but about twenty-four hours before she was killed. So it came down to Jim and Danny. If one of them had killed Francine, he had also killed Mrs. Morton. I couldn't accept that. I had known Jim for years, liked him and felt sorry for him for being fool enough to marry a woman like Francine. Danny was just a boy. But boys of his age could be killers. I thought about all the articles about juvenile delinquents in the newspapers and magazines. Danny was fourteen or fifteen -- just the age when boys were the least stable and the most prone to violence. I could just barely see him as Francine's murderer; I could not see him killing his grandmother. I suppose that was simply prejudice because I liked the boy but he didn't seem to me to be capable of turning murderously on someone he loved.

I put the last stitch in the hem of my dress and knotted it firmly. It was as I was picking up the scissors to clip the thread that an idea so amazing, so revolutionary, hit me that I sat stunned. *Suppose Francine hadn't disappeared but was hiding -- suppose she killed her mother-in-law.* That would account for Jim and Danny behaving as they had. I couldn't think of a good reason for Francine to kill Mrs. Morton, or for her to hide out, but I could see her as a killer much easier than either Jim or Danny. Jim would naturally protect the mother of his children and Danny would protect his father.

How long I sat there, I don't know. It was getting dark when I recoiled from my distressing speculations. I draped the dress over the ironing board for a final pressing and went to the window. The snow was still falling and it seemed to me that it was falling thicker and faster than ever. I needed to make a trip to the bath house so I pulled on my galoshes and slipped into my coat. I thought about locking the door behind me but Uncle Miles' injunctions seemed absurd in the quiet and peacefulness of the fluffy white world around me. I pulled the door to behind me and stood for a moment looking up into the falling snowflakes, letting them settle softly on my face.

Coming back to the house, I was thinking that

129

the dance in Fossil was definitely not on the program that night. There was no way for Guy to reach me and really no need to. We both knew the road conditions. As I opened my door, Danny Morton sprang up from a chair at my kitchen table. I was considerably startled and, frankly, pretty darn scared. Looking at Danny's face, the fear gave way to compassion. The boy was in agony of mind, I couldn't doubt that after I'd got a good look at his face. Still, I stayed at the door.

"I'm sorry, Miss O'Connor. I know I shouldn't have come in when you weren't here but I have to talk to someone."

"What is it, Danny?" I didn't go farther into the room and I guess my voice reflected my fright and suspicion.

"I think I'm going crazy."

He did look on the verge of insanity. Something in my demeanor seemed to strike him. His voice went high-pitched and excited. He was shivering uncontrollably.

"Are you afraid of me, Miss O'Connor?"

I could only nod, dumbly.

"Oh, my God." He flung himself down in a chair and buried his face in his outstretched arms on the table.

"Danny," I said. It came out quavery and I tried

130

again, with better success. "Danny, don't. Sit up and tell me about it."

He looked up. His eyes were dry and there was a twisted sort of smile on his face.

"No wonder Dad thinks I killed Francine and Grandma," he said. "You think so, too."

"No, I don't. Not really. But I'm not sure. How could I be sure?"

He turned that over in his mind and nodded. "I see what you mean. I guess you can't be sure. But I didn't. I never thought of it, even."

"Look, you're nearly frozen. Were you outside all this time? Since noon?"

He nodded. "I went down in the meadow and climbed to the top of the hill in back of it. The snow is so deep it took me a long time."

"Your feet must be wet and frozen."

"Yeah, they are."

"Take off your boots and socks." I took the afghan off the couch and when his feet were bare, I handed it to him. "Wrap your feet up in this."

He did it and I took off my outdoor things.

"You need something hot. Would you rather have tea or coffee?"

"Coffee, please."

I wasn't comfortable turning my back on him but with his feet wrapped up in the afghan, I thought I

131

would have time to run if he started toward me. I didn't really think he was a cold-blooded murderer, but I knew many victims had been surprised by the identity of their assailants. I put the coffee on to perk and got out cups and saucers and spoons. I set a pitcher of cream on the table, along with the sugar bowl.

"I saw you earlier, you know," I told him. "When you ran out of the house and you and your dad were yelling at each other."

"I didn't see you."

"I didn't think you did. You were upset. Well, that's putting it mildly."

"It's been horrible ever since Francine left."

"In what way, Danny?"

I was beginning to trust the boy. I had never really, down deep in my heart believed he was a murderer but seeing him there in my kitchen, seeing how deeply troubled he was, I believed it less and less. He shrugged.

"Oh, you know, everybody's upset and on edge."

The coffee was ready so I poured us each a cup. Danny put sugar and cream in his and stirred it nervously. I sat down and got eye contact with him.

"Danny, do you know where Francine is?"

He tried to keep looking me in the eye but couldn't. He dropped his eyes to his cup and shook

132

his head. He sipped the coffee.

"You don't have any idea?" I applied a little more pressure because I thought he either knew or had a suspicion.

"No. I don't know where she is. I wish my dad had never met the bitch!"

"Danny!"

"I'm sorry." He flicked a look up at me. "I wish my dad hadn't met her. She's been nothing but trouble. He should have stayed with my mom. You don't know my mom, do you?"

"No, I never met her. I've heard that she is a nice woman."

He had stopped shivering but left his coat on. He nodded. "She is. She's great. And she's pretty, too. Lots prettier than Francine. Francine uses all that glop on her face until you can't even see what she really looks like. My mom is beautiful. Dad never should have got mixed up with Francine. Then none of this would have happened."

"What do you mean, Danny? What happened to your grandma -- how is that Francine's fault?"

"I mean, if Dad and Mom had stayed together, there wouldn't have been any Francine and Gramma wouldn't have had to come take care of the girls and she wouldn't have got killed. It used to be so great when it was just the three of us. Dad used to take me

133

fishing and hunting and he and Mom used to go dancing and when he was singing, Mom played the piano in the band and everything was fun."

Danny was holding something back. I couldn't tell if he was protecting his own feelings or if it was something more sinister. He wanted to talk but he only wanted to go so far. I wondered if he had some kind of guilty knowledge.

"What is it you know that's tearing you up? I can see there's something. If you tell me, maybe I can help you."

He looked at me then dropped his gaze again.

"Danny, you can't keep it to yourself forever. If you don't tell what you know, someone else may be hurt. Even killed. Maybe you are in danger. If you don't want to tell me, go with me to Uncle Miles' and tell him."

He shook his head, looking weary and scared and stubborn.

"I can't tell him or you. No one else is in any danger. It's over."

I kept trying but eventually I was convinced that whatever he knew, Danny was not going to tell it. I tried to get him to eat a little something but he said he couldn't, that his stomach was all squeezed up. He began to put his socks and boots on.

"I've got to go home."

With his hand on the doorknob, Danny turned and gave me a bleak smile.

"Thanks for the coffee, Miss O'Connor. I'm sorry I got your floor all wet and messed up your afghan. I'm glad you're not afraid of me anymore."

I tried to smile at him but I don't think it was much of a smile. I know I felt like crying. What an awful thing for a boy to have to deal with. All the adults in his life had deserted him one way or another. I could see that, in addition to his grief for his grandmother and the pain of separation from his mother, he was carrying a load of suspicion that his father was a murderer.

"That's okay," I managed to say. "Listen, Danny, if I can do anything..."

"Goodnight, Miss O'Connor." He went out and pulled the door to behind him. He was lost to view in the snow in six steps.

Chapter 10

Cory Blevens came by to verify that I wasn't expecting to go to the dance that evening. He said the phone lines had been down in Kinzua the night before so he hadn't been able to get through to the police. I told him that Mr. Hamilton had been there and said the phones were still down. He went back to his bunkhouse and I pressed my new dress and hung it in the closet. Then I put away the sewing machine and replaced the knick-knacks and the lamp. By then the iron was cool enough so I put it away and the ironing board. It was supper time then and almost dark out. I wasn't all that hungry but I wanted a little something. I decided to stir up a batch of waffles. I'd found some real maple syrup at the Rexall Drug Store in Heppner and it was delicious. With a glass of milk and some of Aunt Genevieve's home canned pears, it was a fine little supper. And there was enough batter for Sunday breakfast, too.

As I was washing up my dishes, I saw two

figures hurrying along, a flashlight beam bouncing in front of them. It was dark and the snow was still falling fast and visibility was practically nil but they were close to my house and I was sure they were Debbie and Dottie Miller, rushing home for supper. It wasn't until I was drying the dishes and putting them in the cupboard that it occurred to me that they were going away from home, not toward. Probably going to Allstons to spend the evening with Linda, I thought. Then I surveyed the long evening stretching before me. Unless I dropped in on someone, I would have only my thoughts for company and I didn't much relish the idea.

Ordinarily, I find myself pretty good company but with mystery, murder, and suspicion going round and round in my mind, I was wishing for a companion. I didn't want to visit anyone, though. I didn't think I could stand small talk or a game of pinochle and I certainly had no wish to discuss life and death in Camp Five. I sat down cross-legged on the floor in front of my phonograph cabinet to choose some music to listen to. I wanted something calm and soothing, without vocals. I didn't have much along those lines. I finally selected an album that I'd bought at an ice skating show Mom and I had gone to one afternoon in Portland when Daddy was at a Pontiac convention. So my associations with the music were all pleasant and I could picture the skaters in their costumes as I listened. I put a stack of records on the phonograph and turned it on.

There was a half-finished tea cloth in my embroidery basket, a big cluster of flowers in each corner and another in the center. Embroidery almost always had a soothing effect on me and whenever unpleasant thoughts of Francine's disappearance or Mrs. Morton's murder intruded, I swept them firmly away. I thought I'd succeeded pretty well when a scream brought me to my feet, my heart racing. It's just the cougar, I told myself. Calm down. I went to the sink and got a drink of water. Then the scream came again. It was muffled by the thick snowflakes in the air but this time it didn't stop with just one cry.

All at once I knew where it was coming from and who was doing it. Debbie and Dottie! I snatched my coat and wrenched the door open. Not stopping for galoshes, I pulled the coat on as I floundered through the snow. The screaming stopped but I kept on. Mr. Chichester and Cleve Price and Steve Allston came running out of their houses. They were nearest to me and to Jim Morton's and I expect the snow kept the rest of the camp from hearing the noise. Jim came out of his back door as the rest of us converged on it. The men stopped to talk to Jim but I went on past. I think I knew what I was going to find even before I got there because I remember that I felt no surprise at all.

Debbie was kneeling by the hole at the edge of Jim's yard -- one of the boys had fallen into it a couple of days earlier. I had forgotten all about it until I heard the screaming. Dottie was standing beside her sister, holding the flashlight so it illuminated the inside of the hole. They were both staring into the hole with horror. I knew what they saw. Francine Morton.

"Debbie, Dottie. Come away from there," I said.

Both girls looked at me and seemed to dissolve from their horrified rigidity to frightened little girls.

Debbie scrambled to her feet and they both ran to me and hurled themselves against me.

"Oh, Miss O'Connor," Dottie cried.

"It's awful, Miss O'Connor," Debbie sobbed.

I put my arms around them and tried to quiet them as they both told me what they'd found in the hole in Jim's yard.

The men gathered around the hole and looked with thinly veiled hostility at Jim as he came up to them. The back door of Jim's house opened and Danny started to come forward. Jim turned on him.

"Go back, Danny," he shouted furiously. "Go back and take care of your sisters."

"They're asleep," Danny yelled.

Danny kept on coming and Jim went to head him off.

"I said, go back inside," he said angrily, taking hold of Danny's arm.

"I won't." Danny looked scared and shaky but very determined. He pulled away from his father's restraining hand. "I have to see."

The other men watched as Danny moved forward. Jim stood and looked at his son with despair. Danny looked into the hole then looked steadily into the face of each man with a sick sort of questioning shame. Embarrassed, the men flicked glances at Jim and at one another. Danny walked slowly back to the house and went indoors, closing the door softly behind him.

Jim shrugged as if trying to dislodge an intolerably heavy burden and went over to the men. The twins were crying and not talking much. I kept my arms around them and spoke softly to them, much as one speaks to a spooky horse, and making about as much sense.

Steve Allston spoke first. "It's Francine, isn't it, Jim?"

"Yes, it's Francine." Jim sounded tired.

"You know how she got here, Jim?" Carl Chichester asked.

"No. No, I have no idea. I thought she had gone away with Mason Sturdevant."

"We best get her out of there," Cleve Price stated.

Mr. Chichester looked at me.

"I'll take the girls home and tell the Millers what has happened."

The men nodded.

"I'll get a blanket," Mr. Price said. "We'll have to put her in the first aid room, I reckon."

"That's about the size of it," Mr. Allston agreed. "Then someone had better go into Kinzua and call the police."

"The phone line is down," I said. "Or at least it was earlier. That's what Mr. Hamilton said."

"Well, he'll have to be notified, anyway," said Mr. Chichester. "He can call the police whenever they get the phone line fixed. I'll go as soon as we get this taken care of."

The other men agreed and Mr. Price started after a blanket. I shepherded the twins away and back to their own house. The snow continued to fall. My footprints going down to Jim's were already blurred.

Dottie and Debbie burst through their front door, talking at the tops of their voices, completely bewildering their parents. Mr. Miller was sitting in an easy chair, his feet up on a hassock, with a

Reader's Digest condensed book. Mrs. Miller was sitting at a card table putting together a jigsaw puzzle. She hadn't been at it long so there wasn't enough of the pattern showing to tell what the picture was going to be. Seven-year-old Randy was lying on his stomach on the couch, looking at a *Superman* comic book.

Both parents jumped to their feet when we came in. Mrs. Miller shrieked at them to wipe their feet and Mr. Miller demanded to know what was wrong. The girls ran to Mrs. Miller and she embraced them, realizing that they were distraught. Randy sat up, eyeing his sisters with disfavor.

"What is it, Marge?" Mr. Miller looked ready to dash to his daughters' rescue if only someone would tell him wherein the danger lay. "What's wrong with the girls?"

"They've found Francine Morton's body, Mr. Miller."

"Well, so what? What's that got to do with the twins?"

"I mean Debbie and Dottie found her."

"What?" Mrs. Miller turned a shocked face to me. "When? Just now? Where?"

"What have you two yahoos been up to now?" Mr. Miller demanded of his daughters.

"You were supposed to be at the Allstons',

playing with Linda," Mrs. Miller said, as if she were accusing them of something, which she probably was.

"We started to go there," said Debbie. "But on the way we got to talking about that hole in the Mortons' yard that Lyle fell into. You know, Miss O'Connor."

I nodded. "Yes, I remember."

Dottie took up the story. "We thought it was big enough for a woman's body," she began and had to stop and steady herself before she could continue. "So we decided to look in it. It was horrible."

"Mrs. Morton wasn't fat or anything," Debbie explained. "She would fit in a fairly small hole. We had a flashlight, because it was dark."

"Oh, the flashlight," Dottie exclaimed. "We must have left it there. I'll go get it, Dad."

"Never mind the flashlight," Mr. Miller said. "It's the two of you I'm worried about."

"Take off your coats and boots," Mrs. Miller said to the twins.

"You, too, Margie." Mr. Miller held out his hand to take my coat.

I slipped it off and gave it to him. He laid it over the back of a chair and glanced down at my feet.

"Why, you aren't wearing galoshes. Your feet must be frozen," he exclaimed. "Diane, get Margie some warm slippers."

"You girls go hang your coats up and put your overshoes on the back porch," Mrs. Miller directed.

The twins went out through the kitchen to the back porch. Mrs. Miller disappeared into her bedroom and came back with a pair of fuzzy yellow slippers. They looked brand-new.

"I'm okay, Mrs. Miller," I said. "I don't want to mess up your slippers."

"Don't be silly, Marge," she said. "Put them on. I'm going to make something hot to drink and we're going to get to the bottom of this."

I stepped out of my shoes and into the slippers. They were heavenly warm and toasty.

Randy sidled up to his father. "Daddy."

"Yes, son?"

"Daddy, did Dottie and Debbie do something bad?"

"Why, no. Not bad."

"But something bad happened?"

"It seems so, Randy. Your sisters seem to have discovered Mrs. Morton's body."

"But, Daddy, she was in the first aid room at the shop. Mr. Schuyler said so."

Mr. Miller looked at me. I gave him what I hoped was a sympathetic look but offered no help in explaining what to Randy was a conundrum.

"Yes, that's right. This is a different Mrs. Morton."

"How many Mrs. Mortons are there?"

"Only two in Camp Five."

"And they're both dead?"

"Yes, son, they're both dead."

Randy looked at his father for a long moment and then went out to the kitchen. He sat down at the table and watched his mother as she fussed around making cocoa and setting out a plate of Toll House Cookies. Debbie and Dottie, still looking shaken and frightened, came to stand beside the oil heater. They talked to one another softly in Quoskeen. Mr. Miller shot them a quizzical look.

"Come into the kitchen, Marge, and sit down. You girls come, too."

He shooed us to the table and set a chair for me. Mrs. Miller poured the cocoa into cups and set them before us.

"Help yourself to cookies, Marge. I just made them this afternoon," she said.

"Now," Mr. Miller said, "tell us what happened."

"We started to go over to Linda's house," began Dottie.

"But we got to talking on the way," continued Debbie, "about that hole at Mortons' that Lyle fell in."

145

"And we decided to go look and see if it was big enough to hide a lady in," explained Dottie.

"We've been thinking of where she might be and what might have happened to her," said Debbie. "We couldn't think of any reason that anyone would want to kill Mr. Morton's mother except if she knew too much about what happened to his wife."

The twins looked at us doubtfully.

"Okay," Mr. Miller said. "I think we've got that. Although why you should jump to the conclusion that Mrs. Morton was killed on account of Francine Morton is beyond me."

"Because we couldn't think of any other reason for her being killed," Dottie explained patiently. "She was a nice lady. Who would want to kill a nice lady?"

Randy took advantage of the fact that all attention was on his sisters to eat cookies, rapidly and steadily. We all sipped our cocoa and I, for one, was grateful for the comfort of the hot sweet milky chocolate. No other beverage could have soothed us as well as that hot cocoa.

"When we got there," Debbie went on, "we scraped the snow off the canvas and moved the rocks off the edge and pulled the canvas back."

Dottie began to cry and Debbie joined her.

"It was awful," Dottie wailed. "We could see the

top of her head and it was all bashed in and her hair was covered with something icky."

"She was all kind of like she was squatting. One of her hands was in her lap, sort of," Debbie said through her tears.

"That's when I screamed," Dottie said. "When I saw her hand like that."

"All right, girls," said Mrs. Miller. She went to stand between them and put her arms around them. She kissed them and petted them and murmured meaningless little soothing phrases until they quieted.

"That's all," said Debbie when she could speak. "Then Miss O'Connor and Mr. Allston and Mr. Chichester came."

"And Mr. Price," added Dottie. "And Mr. Morton and Danny."

Mr. Miller looked at me.

"I heard a scream," I told them. "At first I thought it was that cougar again but then there were some more screams and I knew it was someone in distress. I grabbed my coat and ran out to see what the trouble was."

"Weren't you scared?" Mrs. Miller asked. "I would have been."

"I didn't really think about it," I said. "I just wanted to find out who was in trouble and see if I

147

could help. I'd seen the girls go by a few minutes earlier. I expect my subconscious thought of them when the screaming started." I shrugged. "Anyone would have done the same. In fact, five men did just that. Everyone who was close enough to hear. The snow absorbed most of the sound, you know, that's why only a few of us heard it. The ones who were closest."

Mr. Miller nodded. "I see. What were they planning to do when you left?"

"They were going to take her to the first aid room and then one of them was going into Kinzua to tell Mr. Hamilton. Cleve Price, I think. The phone lines are down so he can't call the police but, of course, Mr. Hamilton will have to be told."

"Mr. Hamilton was here this afternoon, wasn't he, Marge?" Mrs. Miller asked.

"Yes. He and Uncle Miles came to my house and I told him about finding Mrs. Morton last night." Last night, I thought. Could it possibly have only been last night? I put the thought away from me and concentrated on helping the Millers deal with the effect of all this on their daughters.

"So the road to Kinzua is still open," she said thoughtfully. "Did he say how the road is to Fossil? Or Heppner?"

"He said it's blocked both ways. Ralph is to keep

148

the road to Kinzua plowed and out to the woods but neither Wheeler Country nor Morrow County has enough equipment to keep all the roads plowed. And I suppose there are a lot of accidents to keep the police and the road crews busy." I said that with a catch in my voice. It was only about a year since my parents had died in an accident, though they were boating, not driving.

"We won't get police help tonight, then," Mr. Miller said. "In fact, it might be days before they get here."

We all contemplated that in silence for a few moments. I stood up.

"I think I'd better go tell Uncle Miles," I said. "He'll want to know."

"I'm going to get these youngsters to bed," Mrs. Miller said.

Mr. Miller walked to the front door with me. I changed back into my own shoes and he held my coat for me.

"Wait just a minute, Margie. I'll go with you."

Mrs. Miller and the children trooped through the living room toward the bedrooms.

"Thanks for the use of your slippers, Mrs. Miller," I said. "Goodnight, kids."

The girls and Randy told me goodnight and kept going. Mrs. Miller stopped for a moment.

"You're welcome, Marge. Thank you for taking care of the twins."

"Of course," I said. There had been no need for her to thank me for that. It was no more than anyone would have done.

Mr. Miller got ready and we went out and down the street to Uncle Miles' and Aunt Genevieve's.

Chapter 11

Mr. Miller walked me over to Uncle Miles' and Aunt Genevieve's and went in with me. We sat in the living room and Aunt Genevieve laid her knitting aside when we told her what the twins had found. Both of them were horrified of course.

"What has happened to Camp Five?" Uncle Miles cried out. "We've always been such a happy little community. Hell, we don't even have fist fights here."

Aunt Genevieve said, dryly, "No bar in camp."

Mr. Miller smiled and Uncle Miles shot her a disapproving look. "It isn't funny, Genevieve."

"No, it certainly isn't," she agreed. "Two women murdered in less than a week."

"Was she murdered?" Uncle Miles asked. "Francine Morton?"

Mr. Miller looked at me. I started to say she had been but on second thought I shook my head.

"I don't really know. From the little I could see, she looked as if her head had been battered. I suppose it might have been an accident of some kind."

Aunt Genevieve snorted. "Talk sense, Margie. If it had been an accident, she wouldn't have been stuffed into a hole in the yard."

"I know," I said. "But until there's an autopsy, I don't see how we can just assume it was murder. People do some very strange things sometimes."

"I know they do," retorted Aunt Genevieve. "But they don't jump into holes and pull tarps over themselves and place rocks around the edges to hold the tarp in place."

I opened my mouth but Uncle Miles held up his hand.

"I think, Margie, we're going to have to go on the assumption that she was murdered. If we're wrong, okay, no harm will have been done. But we have to let people know they need to take precautions until we find out exactly what is going on here."

Uncle Miles lit a cigarette and blew a cloud of smoke that seemed to hang like a haze in front of his face for a moment.

Mr. Miller agreed. "It seems to me that we'd better keep all the kids indoors after dark and tell folks to keep a watch for anything out of the ordinary. Until we know who is responsible, we're going to have to suspect everyone just a little."

"I can't believe my friends and neighbors are killers," declared Aunt Genevieve. "I'd as soon suspect myself as anyone here in camp."

Uncle Miles said seriously, "Probably some do suspect us, just a little in the back of their minds."

"That's going too far, Uncle Miles." I was really distressed. "No one could suspect you or Aunt Genevieve or the Millers or the Allstons or the Schuylers. No one here in camp can be the one who killed them."

Mr. Miller gave me a look of pained commiseration. "I know how you feel, Margie, but it's got to be someone here in camp. No one from outside has been able to get in."

"I'm not so sure," I said, argumentatively. "For one thing, we don't know when Francine was killed and for another, just because the police are afraid of a little snow doesn't mean everyone is."

"You've got a point, all right," Uncle Miles said. "Let's see, we know when Francine was first missed. The morning after Halloween, wasn't it? So she must have been killed Halloween night."

Mr. Miller nodded. "And Mrs. Morton was killed two nights later. We do know when she was killed because you found her right away, Margie. It seems to me that we've got to know if Francine was murdered before we go calling on folks with warnings. We have to know what to tell them."

Uncle Miles stubbed out his cigarette. "I'll get my coat and boots and go up to the first aid room with you."

Aunt Genevieve stood up. "I'll go with you."

The men nodded and Uncle Miles went out to the back porch.

"I'm going to go, too," I said.

Aunt Genevieve stopped and turned to look at me. "It's not necessary, Margie. You can wait here. We won't be gone long."

"It is necessary, Aunt Genevieve. I am not going to be left here alone. I don't need to go into the first aid room but I'm going with you."

"Maybe you're right. It might be best if none of us were alone after dark."

She went into her bedroom and came out a minute later, having changed her slippers for shoes. Uncle Miles came in from the back porch wearing his boots and coat and carrying hers. He held her coat over the oil heater while she sat down and put on her galoshes.

"Thanks, Miles," she said as he held the coat while she slipped it on.

That's one of the nicest things about my Uncle Miles, how thoughtful he is of his wife.

"Ready?" asked Mr. Miller.

Receiving replies in the affirmative, he went and held the door open and we all trooped out. Uncle Miles pulled on a cap to keep his bald pate warm. We were a silent little group as we walked through the snow up to the truck shop. There were lights on inside the shop and the little door cut into one of the big doors was standing open. As we got closer we could hear voices, subdued and muffled by the falling snow, but we couldn't make out any words until we got right up to the door.

Mr. Chichester and Steve Allston were talking.

"It doesn't seem right to leave her there on the floor," Mr. Chichester said.

"No, it doesn't," Mr. Allston agreed. "But I don't see what else we can do."

"No, there's nothing else to do. Fold the blanket over to cover her."

Uncle Miles went through the door first, calling out to let the two men know we were coming.

Mr. Allston came out of the first aid room into the shop.

"Oh, it's you," he said. "Carl, the O'Connors are here, and Paul Miller."

Mr. Chichester came to the door of the first aid room. "Good," he said. "Genevieve, maybe you can tell us what made these wounds on Francine's head."

155

"I hope so, Carl," Aunt Genevieve said. "The more facts we have and the fewer conjectures, the better."

I went in last and Mr. Chichester didn't see me at first. When he did, he scowled disapprovingly.

"Marge, you shouldn't be here," he told me. "This is no place for you and you can't do anything to help."

"Let her alone, Carl," Uncle Miles said. "She didn't want to be left by herself for awhile. She's okay."

Mr. Chichester abandoned me then and went back into the first aid room. The others followed him. It was spooky in the truck shop. The only light came from a bare bulb over a section of the workbench and from the first aid room. There were a couple of big Kenworth log trucks more or less taken to pieces and a portable welder and all kinds of belts and tools and hoses hanging on the walls. It was shadowy and too quiet and downright uncanny. I didn't want to stay there, I wanted light and human companionship. But the only light that was immediately available to me was in the first aid room and the human companionship consisted of two corpses and a covey of ersatz detectives. It would have been funny if it hadn't been so tragic.

There was no place to sit so I stood near the door

to the first aid room. They were speaking quietly inside but I could hear perfectly. Too perfectly. Aunt Genevieve apparently probed Francine's head wounds.

"I can't tell too much," she said. "She's frozen and I can't feel how deep these injuries go. You can see the skin is broken because her hair is all matted with blood. I don't know. It looks to me as if she'd been hit two, maybe three times with some kind of club."

I was trying hard not to picture Francine lying on the floor all bunched up in the same position she'd been in when she was stuffed into that dreadful hole.

"Something like a baseball bat?" Mr. Miller asked.

"A baseball bat is too smooth and rounded to have made these wounds. They seem to have been made with something with sharp edges. Not a meat cleaver, I don't mean. A stick of stove wood, maybe. The kind that's cut from a log, not a branch."

"That makes sense," Uncle Miles said. "A branch would be rounded, like a baseball bat." He paused. "She must have been sitting down. The blows came from above and behind."

"Yes," Mr. Chichester said. "She probably never knew who or what hit her."

157

"Thank God for that," said Aunt Genevieve. "Just a minute, I want to look at Mrs. Morton's head." It was quiet for a few minutes, then, "You were right, Miles, she was struck on the back of the head, too. The scalp wasn't cut, though."

A minute later they all came out of the first aid room and Mr. Chichester turned out the light and locked the door.

"Paul and I think we ought to warn everyone," Uncle Miles said. "Keep the kids in after dark and be careful -- lock doors and so forth."

"God A'mighty," exclaimed Mr. Chichester, "we've never locked our doors in Camp Five unless we were going to be gone a week or so. No one locks their doors. Probably don't even have keys for most of them."

"I know," Uncle Miles agreed. "But we seem to have a killer loose."

"I don't see how it could have been an accident," Mr. Miller said. "Not if it came from above and behind. Especially if she was hit more than once."

"Exactly," Aunt Genevieve chimed in. "Someone sneaked up behind her and..."

I gave an involuntary gasp of horror and Aunt Genevieve broke off her description.

"Yes," said Mr. Chichester, "it's an ugly picture. Try not to think about it too much, Margie."

I didn't say anything and neither did the others. Mr. Chichester meant well but he must have known that it would be pretty nearly impossible for any of us to think about anything else until we knew who had killed Francine and her mother-in-law.

"Let's get started warning folks," Mr. Miller said.

As we went out of the shop, the men divided the camp into quarters and each one set out to cover his quadrant. Aunt Genevieve and I went back to her house. She put a kettle on for tea and we sat at the kitchen table.

"I hope this isn't going to scar the twins for life," I said. "Finding Francine like that and all."

Aunt Genevieve set cups and saucers on the table. "Don't you worry about those two, Margie. They'll be all right. They may have bad dreams for a few nights but they're young enough that it's more exciting for them than frightening."

I thought back over my child psychology course and couldn't remember that any situation similar to this one had been discussed. I'd put Aunt Genevieve ahead of any psychologist anyway.

"I expect you're right," I said.

We sat in companionable silence until the teakettle began to shriek. Aunt Genevieve shot me a look of concern when I jumped, startled and frightened by the sudden, though not unexpected,

159

noise. She poured the boiling water over our tea bags and sat down.

"Margie," she said, "something is troubling you. Something more than just the fact of murder. Do you know who it is?"

"No, of course not. If I did, I'd have told you and Uncle Miles. And Mr. Hamilton."

She gazed at me appraisingly. "Then you are afraid to know who it is. You have a strong suspicion and you don't want it to be that person."

I nodded miserably. "I'm afraid it's Jim or Danny. They both act so wild and strange. They used to be close but now they yell at one another all the time."

"Tell me about it, Margie."

So I told her about Danny's nervousness and Jim trying to shush him all the time and about Danny tearing off down into the meadow and how Jim tried to keep him away from the hole where Francine was that night.

"You know what it sounds like to me?" Aunt Genevieve asked, grimly amused.

"No, what?"

"It sounds like they suspect each other."

I thought about it. She was right, that's exactly what it sounded like. I thought about it a few seconds more.

"But if they suspect each other, neither one of them can be guilty," I said.

Aunt Genevieve nodded. "You've been getting all worked up over nothing, Margie."

"But, Aunt Genevieve, Francine must have been killed in her own home. Or near it. She wasn't wearing a coat, just a housedress."

"That's right. I think she must have been killed in her own home. I couldn't see any other injuries except the ones to her head. There was apparently no struggle. She was hit from behind as she was sitting relaxed at home. Maybe at the kitchen table, maybe in her living room."

I stared at Aunt Genevieve. "That's horrible," I whispered. "That's monstrous."

"Yes, it is. It means that if Jim and Danny are both innocent, someone close to them is guilty. Someone that Francine felt at ease with so that she let them get behind her with a club of some kind."

"A stick of stove wood, you said. So simple to dispose of the weapon -- just put it in the trash burner and walk away. No ballistics for the police laboratory to work on, no fingerprints, no nothing. It's positively diabolical."

"And I would have bet anything that there was no such person in Camp Five."

"Maybe not in camp, at that. I don't want to

161

speak ill of the dead, Aunt Genevieve, but Francine was having an affair with Mason Sturdevant. She was also getting under Orville Patterson's skin. There may have been others that we don't know about."

Aunt Genevieve nodded thoughtfully. "Orville was her ex-husband and there were still strong feelings between them, to say the least. I don't see why Mason would want to kill her, unless she had broken with him."

"If she had, it was within the last few days."

"Of course. Otherwise it would have been all over camp."

"I think Mrs. Morton must have been killed because she found out something damaging to whoever killed Francine. Is that how you see it, Aunt Genevieve?"

She nodded. "I don't see how it could have been anything else. She seems to have been a good woman, not given to making trouble. The kind we call a tower of strength in time of need."

I told her about my talks with Betty Chichester and Eloise Troupe. "I know Danny adored her," I added, "and so did Jim. Anyway, I can't believe either of them would kill her. Especially not like that."

"Well, you never know about people. You think

you know someone inside out and then they say or do something that completely amazes you. But I agree that neither Jim nor Danny seems the kind of person who would sneak up behind their nearest and dearest and bash them over the head with a stick of stove wood."

I shuddered. The back door opened and we could hear someone on the back porch. For a second we exchanged terrified glances, then the kitchen door opened and Uncle Miles came in. Aunt Genevieve and I laughed in sheer reaction.

"Well," said Uncle Miles, "I'm glad to find you ladies so jolly."

He sat down and lit a cigarette. Aunt Genevieve set the kettle back on the burner to heat and got an ashtray for Uncle Miles. She put a cup and saucer in front of him and sat down.

"How did people take it?" Aunt Genevieve asked.

"The idea of locking up and keeping the kids in? Some were shocked and some were scared. Probably most were some of each. They saw the sense in it. Noyle Granville wanted to lock Danny and Jim both up."

"He didn't have any supporters, did he?" asked Aunt Genevieve.

"Not that I talked to. It's probably a good thing

we talked to people separately. If we'd asked everyone to a meeting at the Community Hall we might have had problems."

"I never thought of that," I said. "Funny. It seems the obvious thing to do once you've had it broached."

"Maybe," said Uncle Miles. "I still think it's lucky we didn't think of it in time."

The teakettle began to scream and Aunt Genevieve got up and poured hot water over Uncle Miles' tea bag. I pushed my cup toward her and she refilled it and her own. She sat down again and the three of us sat there, dipping our tea bags up and down. It looked so ludicrous that I nearly laughed out loud.

Uncle Miles looked at me very seriously. "Margie, you'd better stay here tonight."

I shook my head. "Thanks, Uncle Miles, but I'll go home."

Aunt Genevieve endeavored to talk some sense into me. As she put it, "Don't be a stubborn little goose, Margie. You'll most likely lie awake all night, scared of every sound and shadow. Stay here and get a good night's rest."

I was grateful for their concern and I badly wanted to stay and be protected. But it would have been sheer cowardice on my part and I couldn't allow that. I told them so.

"You are just like your father, Margie." Uncle Miles was Daddy's younger brother and they had been close all their lives. "He was just as stubborn and headstrong. But be like him in other ways, too, honey. Remember his common sense and intelligence. Don't do anything foolish."

"I won't." I stood up and picked up my coat.

Aunt Genevieve helped me find the left sleeve after I'd got my arm into the right one.

"We're here, if you need us, Margie."

"Thanks. I won't be too proud to yell for help if I need it."

I left them standing arm in arm and went out the front door into the swirling snowflakes. It was appreciably colder than it had been an hour earlier. The flakes seemed to be smaller and drier. My feet and legs were instantly ice cold after the warmth of Aunt Genevieve's kitchen. I plowed through the snow toward home, thanking Heaven that I hadn't far to go. I was so tired that I was sure I would sleep well in spite of everything.

Chapter 12

The lights I'd left on shown out cheerily through the falling flakes. I floundered my way through snow that was now up to my knees, thinking only of getting back to my own hearth and home, getting warm, and falling into bed. I was thankful that I'd left the lights on. I didn't know if I'd have been able to force myself to go into a dark house that night.

As soon as I kicked off my sodden shoes, I locked the door and padded over to the phonograph and turned it off. I should have put the records back in their case but I was simply too tired to bother. I checked the windows and they were as firmly fastened as it was possible to fasten them. The bedroom window was high and small and wasn't built to open, anyway; ditto the window over the kitchen sink. But the living room windows were sash type and could be opened by pushing the catch back with a knife, once the screen was loosened, which was also easily accomplished with a knife. I didn't like the way my mind seemed to be dwelling on knives but again I was too tired to bother. Anyway, neither of our murders had involved knives.

I felt silly as I did it, but I looked under my bed and in my closet, poking clear to the walls on every side. Leaving all the lights on, I undressed, pulled my flannel pajamas on, opened my bedroom door so no one could sneak up on me, and collapsed into bed. But not to sleep at once. I hadn't really expected to, although I was tired enough to sleep for a week. But seeing Francine's body crouching in that hole in the ground had done terrible things to my equanimity. My world had always been safe and secure, a place where such things didn't happen. When my parents had been killed in that boating accident, I had been torn by grief. I had felt lost and alone. But the world hadn't changed. The neighbors remained the same ordinary, kindly people they had always been. The laws of cause and effect had been seen to operate in an orderly fashion even though the result was so painful. Although I had felt that God might have taken better care of my parents and me, I had not felt that He was too remote to involve Himself in my affairs.

Now I was enmeshed in a world of murder, suspicion, and distrust. I didn't know which of my neighbors were really ordinary and kindly and which was the one who took to murder to accomplish his ends. I didn't even know what the desired end was. I didn't know what the cause was, only the effect. I didn't know for sure which was the primary murder. I thought it must be Francine and that Mrs. Morton had been killed because of something she found out about Francine's murder. But I didn't actually know that.

I was caught in a sort of quicksand of the mind -- every thought flopped around and finally mired in uncertainty. Or maybe it was more like a Ferris wheel. Every thought climbed up and around to the zenith and then slid down and around to the nadir, completing the circle. Up and around, down and around. And all the while gaudily colored lights and bold calliope music distracted me from the simple logic of cause and effect.

If Francine's murder was the primary one, and I couldn't see any real alternative, there must be a cause. Whatever it was that she said or did to arouse murderous fury in someone's breast, it had to be something that left evidence, marks of its existence. Strange that emotions should be strong enough to cause one human being to kill another. I thought of the people I knew who had been deeply emotionally involved with Francine. Her ex-husband, Orville Patterson. Her lover, Mason Sturdevant. Her present

168

husband, Jim Morton. Reluctantly, I added Danny Morton to the list. I could think of two reasons for Danny to kill Francine. The first would be to rid his father of a woman he felt was ruining Jim's life. The other would be to rid himself of a woman he felt had ruined his own life and/or his mother's life -- revenge, in fact, for breaking up his home. Teenage boys sometimes went off the rails and committed murders for such reasons. At least, so the magazine writers said. I wasn't really convinced but supposed it could be so.

That pretty well exhausted my roster of suspects. There might be other men of whom I had no knowledge. In fact, given Francine's personality and character -- or lack of character -- there were almost certainly others who had reason to wish her out of the world. Aunt Genevieve and I had given each other reasons why neither Jim nor Danny could be guilty. At the time they had seemed cogent and convincing. Now, in the middle of the night, they smacked of rationalization. I began again. Mason Sturdevant lived in Kinzua and if he had been in camp the night Francine was killed, someone would have known it and commented on it. The fact would have been known to every household within twenty-four hours. The same went for Orville Patterson, who also lived in Kinzua. Or did it? I suddenly remembered the car I'd heard start up while I was picking porcupine quills out of my stomach. That could have been either Orville or Mason. Or neither.

The clock registered 12:46 a.m. I got up and slipped my feet into house shoes. Wrapping myself in a warm chenille robe, I went into the kitchen end of my front room and put a little milk in a saucepan to heat. I wished I had some sleeping pills. Then I knew it didn't matter because I would be afraid to take them. I wanted some sleep but I also wanted the ability to come instantly awake with all my faculties about me in case there was any danger lurking out there in the dark. It was at that point that I realized I needed to make a trip to the bath house.

I looked out the window and could only see that it was still snowing thickly. Although we got snow often at Camp Five, it seldom got more than a foot or so deep. And it never snowed so much so early in the year. I was beginning to envision it piling up to thirty or forty feet as it did in places like Crater Lake in the Cascades. We would have to tunnel our way from door to door. The woods would be shut down and the men would have to stay in camp all day every day. That would be something. I tried to envision a hundred people with simultaneous cabin fever. It was not a pretty picture.

Yanking myself out of these daydreams and

back to reality, I pulled on my overshoes and coat. I turned the heat off under the milk and steeled myself to open the door and step out into the dark and the cold. I thought about taking the flashlight but didn't. It wouldn't be much help in seeing through the snow and might give me away to anyone watching. Not that I really believed anyone was watching. Why would they? If anyone seriously wanted to kill me, all they had to do was come to my door, break out the window, reach in and turn the knob, and do it. I think the shadow of a chipmunk scurrying across the snow would have sent me into hysteria just then but, thankfully, no shadow materialized. With the bravado of desperation, I opened the door and dashed across to the women's bath house. It was cold inside, the company only keeping enough heat in it to prevent the pipes from freezing. I was shivering as much with cold as with fright as I washed my hands and hurried back across the snow to my house.

It was a tremendous relief to step back into the warmth of home. It seemed to wrap itself around me like a down-filled quilt. I repeated my search under the bed and in the closet before I took off my outdoor things. Then I turned on the burner under the milk and made the cocoa.

I felt too exposed for comfort in the front room,

so I took my cocoa into my bedroom and drank it in bed with a heavy sweater over my shoulders and my feet on the heating pad. While I was sipping the cocoa, I decided to take Mr. Hamilton's suggestion to write everything down that I thought could possibly relate to the murders. It was almost 2:30 when I finished. It was highly unsatisfactory, not adding a thing that I could see to the elucidation of our mysteries.

Exhausted, I instructed my mind to settle down for the night and let me alone. I curled up under the covers and finally fell into an uneasy light sleep. I jerked awake to listen, with my heart thumping in my chest. At first I wasn't sure if I had heard a noise or if I'd been dreaming. Then, suddenly, the answer was there. I had no doubt that it was the right answer but I knew I had to be able to set forth my reasons for believing it before anyone else would take it seriously. I grabbed my notebook and pen and wrote feverishly.

Carleen. Carleen, who'd had a crush on Jim since she was in high school. Carleen, who could not bear to be less than first in anything. Carleen, who had made at least two trips to camp during the last week. I made a chart incorporating all the facts I had and the time table. The only name that fit everywhere was Carleen. I laid the notebook and pen on the bed and decided to sit up the rest of the night. I also resolved to get a hand gun the first chance I got.

It was hard to believe at first. I'd known Carleen since we were children and my cousin Lorraine and I had played paper dolls and jacks with her. I'd known her all through our high school years, mostly in the summer, as she and Lorraine had gone to high school in Fossil and I'd gone in Heppner. But I knew her well and knew that she could never tolerate losing -- not at jacks, not at adolescent dating games. Apparently, she had decided not to tolerate losing Jim to Francine.

I faltered then. Would anyone kill in order to clear the way to a man's heart? Jealousy was a powerful motive, I knew that. But was it powerful enough to murder a man's wife and his mother? It had to be the same motive for both women. Mrs. Morton hadn't been there when Francine was killed and dumped in the hole in the ground. So she couldn't have seen or heard anything that would have endangered the killer. And if she had found incriminating evidence, she would have at least told her son about it and he clearly suspected Danny.

Carleen's attitude to me as Jim and I had passed through his kitchen as she was fixing his lunch was all at once crystal clear. I had sensed her hostility at the time but had been vaguely puzzled by it. Concern for Jim and Danny and the babies had put it out of my mind but now it flooded back. Carleen had begun to wonder if there was an attachment between Jim and me. I shivered although I was toasty warm.

At the sound of the crummies starting up at 5:00, I crawled out of bed drearily, tired and unrefreshed, wondering if I could possibly be right about Carleen. It seemed very unlikely in the light of day. I glanced out the window and saw that it was no longer snowing. That lifted my spirits somewhat. Soon the state police would be able to get to camp and we could get back to normal living. Right or wrong, and I knew I was right, I couldn't see that anyone else posed a threat to Carleen or that there was anything I could do until the police arrived. Meanwhile, I might as well go to school.

I made my bed and put the notebook and pen on the dresser. I made some coffee and fixed a bowl of oatmeal. I don't know of any breakfast that is more normal and comforting than oatmeal. I wasn't my usual perky self by any means as I started down the hill to school, but my mind was not as inert and foggy as it had felt when I first woke up. Although the day was sunny, the temperature was, if anything, colder than when it was snowing. It felt much more

174

like a midwinter day than a late autumn day. The world was very beautiful with its smooth covering of glittering white.

The children were alternately subdued and rambunctious. The weather made them effervescent but the murders frightened them. So it wasn't a very illuminating day and I'm not sure that I taught anyone anything whatever. Debbie and Dottie Miller were extremely trying with their whispered conferences in Quoskeen, whenever they thought I was absorbed with someone else. Ray Troupe and Lyle Allston took every opportunity to try to trip one another or bump one another so they would have an excuse to fight at recess. Doreen Cranston giggled almost incessantly, totally without cause, as far as I could tell. I was quite surprised to have Twyla Schuyler burst into tears when I asked her to come up to the board and diagram a simple declarative sentence. By the time I'd got her calmed down, it was lunch time.

A bowl of vegetable soup with crackers and hot tea gave me enough energy to go back to school. My head was fuzzy from lack of sleep and the strain of the past three days. Only three days? My mind rebelled at the thought of cramming everything that had happened into a mere three days. The walk in the cold air, short as it was, put a little spring in my

175

step. By the time I got to the porch, I was feeling almost alert. I couldn't remember whose turn it was to blow the whistle so I blew it myself.

The children trooped in, stomping the snow off their galoshes, hanging up their coats and caps, and making enough noise for triple their number. They finally settled into their seats and I picked up the book I was reading aloud to them. I guess the rest of the afternoon went okay. I don't really remember most of it. I handed out the papers I'd corrected and Debbie and Dottie turned in their report on weather. I gave each class their spelling assignments for the week and gave the fifth, sixth, and eighth grades reading assignments. Then I took the four seventh graders to the board to work on decimals. Math was not my strong suit and I had never really understood the advanced branches but decimals were pretty straight forward. I was getting frustrated with Cynthia Masour's questions. Darla Ziegler decided to explain but since she didn't understand decimals, either, it got pretty confusing.

I had a raging headache by the time I left seventh grade math and embarked on fifth grade history. Both Debbie and Dottie knew more about the Louisiana Purchase than I did and I rather resented it that afternoon. All in all, I was heartily glad when the hands of the clock finally clicked around to

3:30. The kids clattered and slammed their way out to the porch and on outside. I laid my head on my arms and I think I could have gone to sleep right there at my desk.

The door from the community hall/gym opened behind me and I spun around, ready to run and then relaxed as I saw it was Sylvia Ziegler.

Sylvia smiled wryly. "Nerves are strung up pretty tightly, aren't they, Marge?"

I nodded. "Sure are. How about you? How are your nerves?"

"I'm okay. I just looked in to say that I'm going now. I'll lock the door to the hall and, of course, my classroom door."

"Thanks. I'll lock the front door. I'm going in a minute or two."

"See you tomorrow."

Sylvia went back through the community hall, closing my door behind her. I sat staring out the window at the glittering snow on the meadow, on the trees on the hillside behind it. It was so very lovely. Then a picture of Mrs. Morton lying on the sled in the snow popped into my mind. I jumped to my feet, scooping up a stack of papers to take home for grading. The porch door opened and Carleen Chichester, that is, Carleen Burch came in. She was wearing a long woolen coat and had a brightly colored scarf tied over her head. She looked very pretty and merry. Except for the double-barreled 12-gauge shotgun she pulled out from under her coat. I must have looked like a cretin because she smiled faintly and told me to close my mouth.

"You always were naive," she said, "even when we were little girls, you knew less about everything than anyone else."

My mind was not asking questions, it was not even making comments. All it was doing was registering the fact of Carleen and the shotgun.

Carleen laughed lightly. "I can't see what Jim could possibly see in a nebbish like you," she said. Her voice hardened, "I went to your house this afternoon. I found some very interesting reading in that notebook on your dresser."

I must have looked as blank as I felt because she frowned. "Don't be such a dope, Marge."

She began to lift the shotgun to her shoulder.

"Wait." I suppose that was just as idiotic as Carleen expected but I wanted to get things clear in my mind. If I had to die -- and even with a pistol or a rifle, let alone a shotgun, in Carleen's hands at that range there wasn't any doubt that I did have to die -- I wanted to understand why. "You really did kill Francine? And Mrs. Morton?"

Carleen shook her head, the way people do

shake their heads when stupidity reaches a certain incredible level. "Yes. Yes, Marge, that's what I mean. I killed Francine. I hit her with a stick of firewood, you know. Several times. Then I put the wood in the trash burner. Very neat and tidy. It was overcast and almost dark, so I knew I wouldn't be seen. The men hadn't come home yet and everyone else was inside that time of day, getting supper ready for them. I dragged her out and dropped her in that hole Jim dug to get at the water line. He was going to put a hydrant in that corner of the yard. Francine wanted to make a flower bed over there and Jim wanted to make it easy for her to water it." Carleen laughed shortly. "Okay? Now is it all clear?"

Moronically, I nodded and she began to raise the shotgun again. The door behind Carleen flew open and she whirled around, leveling the shotgun as she turned. She fired without waiting to see who had burst into the room. But Danny Morton hadn't come in to see what was going on, he had come to stop what he was afraid was going on. He flung the door open and made a diving tackle, bringing Carleen down with a thud. One barrel of the 12-gauge sprayed shot in the outer porch door. The noise was deafening in that enclosed space. Carleen was a fighter and had lost all the good sense she ever had.

Finding she couldn't kick herself free of Danny's grip on her legs, she twisted around to club him with the butt.

By that time I had more or less come to my senses. I scrambled around my desk and down the aisle between the fifth and sixth grades, running into desks and shoving them out of my way. Carleen heard me and brought the shotgun around to point at me. I tried to drop down behind one of the desks but I wasn't quick enough. I heard the blast of the second barrel as I hit the floor.

Danny was yelling something and Carleen was screaming and crying with rage and frustration. All at once it was quiet. I sat up to see what was happening. Danny was getting to his feet and Carleen was lying prone and still. I tried to stand up and was stopped by searing pain in my right shoulder. I looked down to see blood spreading across my shoulder and running down my side.

"Damn it," I said, "my blouse is ruined." Then the pain slammed into me and I burst into tears.

A couple of hours later I was lying back in Uncle Miles' recliner chair, wrapped in Aunt Genevieve's warmest quilted bathrobe, feeling fine except for my shoulder. Aunt Genevieve had cleaned my wound and bandaged it, after giving me the strongest pain killer she had, some kind of

180

codeine, I guess. So the shoulder didn't hurt much unless I moved it and I wasn't going to move it unless I had to.

Danny had already explained to Aunt Genevieve and me how he happened to be johnny-on-the-spot but when the men came back from work, Uncle Miles demanded the whole story right from the horse's mouth. So Danny had been sent for and was sitting on the couch with Max and Sylvia Ziegler while Uncle Miles and Aunt Genevieve sat in easy chairs opposite them. All the grown-ups but me had highballs. Danny had a glass of 7-Up and I had a cup of tea with a big dollop of honey that I had no intention of drinking. I detest honey in tea. But Aunt Genevieve said it would be good for me, what with the shock and all.

Sylvia told how the sound of the shotgun blasts had brought her running back to the school. It had brought a good many other people, as well, but she got there first. Danny had sent her to see to his sisters, his father having left him baby-sitting.

"The girls were all alone, you see, and someone had to stay with them. Misty was in her bassinet but Holly was playing with her blocks in the living room. She likes to stack them just as high as she can and then she laughs and claps when they fall over."

"Yes," said Uncle Miles. "We realize that

someone had to stay with the babies. How did you know that Margie needed help?"

"Well, I didn't, really. But since the road to Fossil was still snowed in this morning, I couldn't go to school. Dad had gone to Kinzua to see if the phone line had been fixed so he could call the funeral home. And I happened to glance out the living room window and see Mrs. Burch going into the school. I couldn't see any reason she should be going to the school. I mean, she doesn't have any kids. I knew she was a nut case and there was something funny about the way she was walking -- sort of stiff. I just thought I'd better see if Miss O'Connor needed any help."

Uncle Miles gave me a look as if to ask if this made any sense to me. I smiled at him and he gave a different kind of look, as if he was dubious about letting me stay up with the grown-ups.

"Danny, what do you mean Mrs. Burch was a nut case?" Sylvia asked.

"She was always hanging around our place, especially after Francine disappeared." He shrugged. "I never paid much attention to her; I just thought she was a dreary old bat. She followed Dad around like he was Bo-Peep and she was a lamb. Francine used to make fun of her. Not to her face, of course, but to Dad and me."

182

Aunt Genevieve gave him a long, appraising look. "Did you know that she killed Francine?"

Danny looked guilty and sheepish. "No. It never crossed my mind until I heard some of what she was saying to Miss O'Connor this afternoon."

"You thought Jim had, didn't you, Danny?" I asked.

He nodded reluctantly. "I kind of did. See, I saw him the night Francine disappeared. He was out by the back door and I could see him clubbing something. The bedroom window is too high to see much but I could see his arm going up and down and he had some kind of stick in his hand. The next morning there was blood all over the place out there. And there was an axe handle in the garage that had blood all over one end of it. I cut it in pieces and put it in the trash burner. I still don't know what that was all about. I couldn't ask him." Danny spoke as if through a lot of anguish.

"I wish I'd known," I said. "I could have saved you a considerable amount of suffering."

Everyone turned puzzled faces toward me.

"I fell over a porcupine that night," I explained. "Jim picked me up and took me home. He must have killed the porky when he went back. That's what you were doing that next day," I said to Danny, "when I came over and found you scraping

183

snow off the back step and around it. I couldn't figure out what you were up to."

"Well, I was cleaning up the blood, of course."

Uncle Miles snorted. "I think you'd better learn to observe a little closer. There must have been quills scattered around and footprints to show what had happened."

Danny flicked a look at Uncle Miles. "I just wanted to get it cleaned up quick. The light wasn't very good and, of course, the whole area around there was pretty much trampled. Anyway, I never thought of sorting out the footprints. I just wanted to get the blood cleaned up."

"We all understand that, Danny, and we don't fault you for it, either." Aunt Genevieve glanced at the others; the Zieglers both nodded. "Family has to stick together."

"I still don't see what made you go to the school," Max Ziegler said. "Even if Carleen doesn't have kids, she and Marge grew up together. It wouldn't be that out of the way for her to drop in for a visit."

"That's just it, sir. I'd heard her talking a lot and I knew that she didn't like Miss O'Connor." Danny shot an apologetic glance at me. "And, like I said, I knew she was nuts. I just thought I'd better go see that it was all right."

"I was never so glad to see anyone in my life," I declared. "That was the cleanest tackle I've ever seen. Pow! Down she went." I sent Danny an admiring look but then I turned thoughtful. "That didn't knock her out, though. She tried to club you with the 12-gauge after that and she shot me. What knocked her out?"

Danny was looking apologetic again and very earnest. "I did. I know guys shouldn't hit women but I couldn't think of anything else to do so I gave her a right uppercut. I was all off balance, though, and I couldn't get a good solid shot at her. I think she must have had a glass jaw or something."

He stared in disapproving amazement as the five of us laughed until we cried.

About the Author

Barbara J. Olexer is a fourth-generation Oregonian. She has written more than twenty books and screenplays. Her first published book was *The Enslavement of the American Indian*, a nonfiction account of that little-known segment of American history.

Her formative years were spent in small farming towns and a backwoods logging camp. Barbara's life has been a tapestry of changes as she has lived and worked in small Oregon towns, such as Ashland, Camp Five (a logging camp that belonged to Kinzua Pine Mills), Klamath Falls, and Malin, as well as some of the country's biggest cities, such as San Francisco, Hollywood, Baltimore, and Washington, D.C.

On retirement, Barbara returned to the Pacific Northwest where her two grown sons and her grandchildren live. She lives in Milwaukie, Oregon, with her husband and two cats.

63647019R00105